"We're a lot alike, Sidney. Workaholics with no sense of time or place."

She smiled. "And here I was thinking how different we are."

"In what way?"

"You're at home any place in the world. I'm only happy when I'm here in Devil's Cove. You willingly put yourself in harm's way for the sake of your job. I'm the biggest coward in the world. I can't imagine having the courage to face down danger over and over again."

"But what about the perils of everyday life? There are different degrees of danger. You never know how much courage you have until you're called upon to face a challenge."

He took her empty mug from her hand and gathered her into his arms. "Enough talk about how alike or different we are. There's one thing we can absolutely agree on."

Whatever she'd been about to say was gone from her mind in an instant as, with one kiss, one touch, she lost herself in the pleasure he offered....

Dear Reader,

The weather's hot, and so are all six of this month's Silhouette Intimate Moments books. We have a real focus on miniseries this time around, starting with the last in Ruth Langan's DEVIL'S COVE quartet, *Retribution*. Mix a hero looking to heal his battered soul, a heroine who gives him a reason to smile again and a whole lot of danger, and you've got a recipe for irresistible reading.

Linda Turner's back—after *way* too long—with the first of her new miniseries, TURNING POINTS. A beautiful photographer who caught the wrong person in her lens has no choice but to ask the cops—make that *one particular cop*—for help, and now both her life and her heart are in danger of being lost. FAMILY SECRETS: THE NEXT GENERATION continues with Marie Ferrarella's *Immovable Objects,* featuring a heroine who walks the line between legal, illegal—and love. *Dangerous Deception* from Kylie Brant continues THE TREMAINE TRADITION of mixing suspense and romance—not to mention sensuality— in doses no reader will want to resist. And don't miss our stand-alone titles, either. Cindy Dees introduces you to *A Gentleman and A Soldier* in a military reunion romance that will have your heart pounding and your fingers turning the pages as fast as they can. Finally, welcome Mary Buckham, whose debut novel, *The Makeover Mission,* takes a plain Jane and turns her into a princess—literally. Problem is, this princess is in danger, and now so is Jane.

Enjoy them all—and come back next month for the best in romantic excitement, only from Silhouette Intimate Moments.

Yours,

Leslie J. Wainger
Executive Editor

Please address questions and book requests to:
Silhouette Reader Service
U.S.: 3010 Walden Ave., P.O. Box 1325, Buffalo, NY 14269
Canadian: P.O. Box 609, Fort Erie, Ont. L2A 5X3

RUTH LANGAN
Retribution

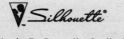

INTIMATE MOMENTS™

Published by Silhouette Books

America's Publisher of Contemporary Romance

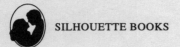

SILHOUETTE BOOKS

ISBN 0-373-27373-8

RETRIBUTION

Copyright © 2004 by Ruth Ryan Langan

This edition published by arrangement with Harlequin Books S.A.

® and TM are trademarks of Harlequin Books S.A., used under license.
Trademarks indicated with ® are registered in the United States Patent
and Trademark Office, the Canadian Trade Marks Office and in other
countries.

Visit Silhouette Books at www.eHarlequin.com

Printed in U.S.A.

Books by Ruth Langan

RUTH LANGAN

is an award-winning and bestselling author of contemporary and historical romance. Her books have been finalists for the Romance Writers of America's (RWA) RITA® Award. Over the years, she has given dozens of print, radio and TV interviews, including *Good Morning America* and *CNN News,* and has been quoted in such diverse publications as the *Wall Street Journal, Cosmopolitan* and the *Detroit Free Press.* Married to her childhood sweetheart, she has raised five children and lives in Michigan, the state where she was born and raised. Ruth enjoys hearing from her readers. Letters can be sent via e-mail to ryanlangan@aol.com or via her Web site at www.ryanlangan.com.

To Tom, with love

Prologue

Sidney Brennan worked quickly to catch the last rays of the fading sunlight that fanned over the pale, sun-washed landscape. The distant villa, with its stucco walls and tiled roof, was framed with those long rows of grapevines that grew in such profusion. She mixed the paints on her palette until she had the perfect shade of light that tinted the hills surrounding the village in hues of terra-cotta and burnt umber.

At last she set down her paints and took a moment to assess her work. Though she'd captured the feeling of the place where she was staying, the painting didn't move her. Instead, it left her feeling empty.

Like her life. Like her heart. Like her future.

The best that could be said about it was that it was merely adequate. There was no passion. No fire. Anyone looking at it would recognize this place. But would they feel the burning desire to live here? Did the painting call to them?

What was calling to her was food. She touched a hand to her middle and realized she'd forgotten to eat. Again. Picking up the canvas and paints, the easel and stool, she lugged them across the field and stowed them just inside the door of the villa before going to the kitchen in search of food. Half an hour later she sat on a little balcony and nibbled cheese and bread, washing it down with wine while she watched the sun set over those glorious, purple-hued hills.

This lovely old villa in Tuscany was to have been her haven while her heart healed and she immersed herself in the great passion of her life. She'd come to this place to follow a dream. Instead, it had become her prison. The solitude she had always enjoyed was now filled with utter loneliness. She was bedeviled with memories. Memories that had begun to affect her work. Though she was perfectly capable of capturing the light, the scenery, the feelings of this place, there was no denying that the work she was turning out was mediocre at best.

Sipping her wine she closed her eyes to the beauty around her and drifted back to the month before graduating college.

* * *

Silver mylar balloons floated above the hospital bed, anchored by an ice bucket painted with a happy face. Champagne and tulip glasses were cooling on ice. The groom-to-be, too weak to stand, lay surrounded by pillows. He wore a tuxedo jacket over his hospital gown, with a white rosebud pinned to his lapel. His mother and father stood beside the bed, exchanging anxious, worried looks.

The entire Brennan family was there. Judge Frank Brennan, who would perform the ceremony, stood beside his wife Alberta, whom everybody called Bert. Their daughter-in-law Charlotte, nicknamed Charley, stood with her daughters Emily, Hannah and Courtney, dressed in pale pink confections that made them look like prom queens. ''The Wedding March'' drifted over the intercom, and patients and their families stood in the doorways of their rooms to watch as the young bride, dressed in a traditional white-lace gown, walked slowly along the hallway on the arm of her father, Dr. Christopher Brennan. As they progressed to the groom's bed, those on the cardiac floor who were mobile followed, until the room and the hallway outside were filled to overflowing with curious onlookers.

The bride settled herself on the edge of the bed beside her husband-to-be, and handed her bouquet to her sister, Emily. When the music ended, the young couple joined hands.

*The judge cleared his throat. "Dearly beloved."
He swallowed the lump that threatened, and forced
himself to continue in a strong clear voice. "We are
gathered together for the most joyous of occasions.
The union of this man to this woman in holy mat-
rimony." He closed his book and glanced around.
"Sidney and Curt have written their own ceremony,
and ask only that we share this moment and offer
our blessings."*

*He nodded at the young couple, who were staring
into each other's eyes with matching looks of love
and wonderment.*

*The groom-to-be spoke first in halting tones, paus-
ing often for a wheezing breath. Beside him, a machine gave off blips that matched his erratic heart-
beats.*

*"Sidney, the first time I saw you, with that red
hair flowing down your back and those eyes as
green as shamrocks, I was determined to get to know
you. I figured I didn't stand a chance, since you
were the most popular student on campus. But after
one meeting, I knew that I wanted more than friendship. I sensed that you were fated to be my wife."*

*Sidney smiled. "I can top that. I fell in love with
you before I even saw you. I remember seeing a
bronze sculpture of three little ducklings. One had
just fallen off a curb, and the other two were poised,
as though to follow. I was so enchanted by the work,
I stood there for an hour or more, marveling at the*

fact that I could almost feel their downy feathers and hear their little quacks of distress. And then a week later I met the artist, and I knew I'd met my soul mate."

He lifted her hand to his lips. *"This isn't exactly the way I'd planned our wedding. And certainly not what I'd hoped for our future. But I'm grateful for the time we've had."* He closed his eyes, as though even that small effort cost too much. *"You've given my life meaning, Sidney. Just knowing you, loving you and knowing you love me, is enough for a lifetime."*

His hand released its grip on hers and fell limply at his side. Sidney leaned over to brush a kiss on his lips and felt the lack of response. At the same instant a machine beside the bed began emitting one long continuous beep. It was, to Sidney's ears, the most chilling sound she'd ever heard.

Dr. Christopher Brennan shoved his way toward the bed, touching a hand to his patient's chest. When he looked up, his eyes met his wife's.

She put her arms around their daughter, gathering her close as Christopher gave a shake of his head. *"I'm sorry. We thought there might be enough time. But it's…too late."*

Curt's mother was weeping while his father stood beside her, looking lost and helpless.

A nurse began hustling the others from the room. Before the family could make their exit, Sidney *caught her grandfather's arm. "Wait, Poppie. Say the words. I need...I need to hear the words that would have made us husband and wife."*

The old man arched an eyebrow and glanced at his wife. At her little nod he cleared his throat. The book in his hand was forgotten. Now he would simply improvise, and hope he could find something to say that might ease the pain of the moment for all of them, but especially for this sweet, beloved granddaughter who had always seemed more delicate, more fragile than her sisters. The depth of her pain and grief tore at his heart.

"We have all witnessed the two of you pledge your love to one another. It matters not whether you had the opportunity to be joined as husband and wife, but rather that your intentions were true. It matters not that one heart stopped, for the other heart is strong enough for two. And so I declare, by the power vested in me, that the pledge made this day will be remembered by all assembled here, as it will be recorded, I'm sure, in both your hearts for all time."

Sidney opened her eyes. The Tuscany landscape was now steeped in shadow. The air had grown cooler, forcing her to draw a shawl around her shoulders.

She'd come here because it had been Curt's dream. It was all he'd talked about. Her graduation, their marriage and the year they would spend in this lush, lovely place, living in an ancient villa that belonged to a friend of the family, while studying the masters.

Poppie was fond of saying that plans were what people made while real life was happening around them.

The realization came slowly, like the light fading behind the craggy mountain peaks in the distance. She couldn't go on living Curt's dreams. She had to live her own. In the real world.

She needed to go home to her family. Back to Devil's Cove. To paint the things she'd always loved. Nature. Wildlife. Especially waterfowl. Wasn't that what had first attracted her to Curt? The fact that they shared a love of art, a love of waterfowl, and their delightful antics had been a special bond between them.

For the first time in a year she felt a stirring of hope. Of life. Curt was gone, and the pain of that loss would never leave her. But the dream lived on. Only now, it must be her dream. Her choice. Her future.

She must face it alone.

Chapter 1

Devil's Cove—Present Day

"I know, Picasso. You're always in a hurry." Sidney looked over at the scrawny mutt with gray, wiry hair that made him look like a cross between a steel-wool scrubbing pad and a wire brush. She'd found him cowering in the woods the previous winter, and was delighted when her ad in the local newspaper had produced no one interested in claiming him, for the truth was that this poor, bedraggled little dog had stolen her heart. "Why can't you be serene like Toulouse?"

The object of her praise, a black-and-white tabby that had wandered in several months ago and had made himself at home, was busy weaving figure eights between the dog's legs. Odd, Sidney thought, that these two different animals had formed an instant bond. As though each recognized in the other a kindred spirit. The lost and lonely, seeking love and the comfort of home, someone to tend to their needs.

But while she was tending them, she realized they were filling a need in her, as well. They might be just two little animals, but they were someone to talk to in the silence of the day. Warm bodies in the darkness of the night. Boon companions to whom she could confide her most intimate secrets, without fear of ever having them revealed to others. Their companionship eased the enforced loneliness that had become a necessary part of her life.

''All right. I know it's time to go.'' With a sigh, Sidney drained the last of her coffee and set the cup in the dishwasher before picking up her easel and canvas, a wooden case that held her paints and brushes and a small folding stool. All of these were placed in an old wooden wagon.

The minute she opened the door, the dog and cat ran ahead, ready for another day of adventure.

''Oh, sure. Once we're outside, you never wait for me.'' With a laugh she closed the door to the little cabin that she now called home.

When she'd first returned to Devil's Cove, she'd lived at the Willows, the lovely old mansion overlooking Lake Michigan that had been her family's home for more than fifty years. That was where her grandparents lived, and where her mother had first come as a bride, with her father. It was where they had raised their four daughters, and where each of Sidney's sisters had lived until finding a home of their own.

For the first few months Sidney had welcomed the tender ministrations of her family. The serene walks along the shore with Bert. The long, late-night talks with Poppie in his study. And the determination of Trudy, their lifelong housekeeper, to, as she had said in that wonderful old rusty-gate voice, ''ply her with food and put some weight on her bones.'' But before long Sidney had recognized the worried looks, the questioning glances that passed between her family members. Their constant hovering had begun to make her feel helpless and more than a little smothered. Despite the fact that she was still grieving, and feeling confused about how to get on with her life, she recognized that it would be far too easy to become dependent upon her family for the strengths she needed to find within herself.

''Not yet, dear,'' Bert had said gently when Sidney first mentioned finding a place of her own. ''It's too soon. Your emotions are still too raw. Let us indulge you a while longer.''

''Besides,'' Poppie had said a bit more vehemently. "Who would stay up late with me and argue the latest murder cases being aired on the news?"

"If you go," Trudy said in that raspy voice roughened by years of smoking, "your grandfather will be forced to eat an entire batch of chocolate-chip cookies by himself. And then his cholesterol will go up, and his blood pressure, and who knows what else?"

Sidney had remained adamant. "I won't be bribed or made to feel guilty about going. It's time."

Once she'd begun seriously shopping for a place to call her own, her mother, Charley, a real-estate agent, had discovered this little cabin in the woods. From the moment Sidney set foot inside, she'd known it was meant to be.

She still felt a thrill each time she returned home. She loved everything about it. The way it sat, snug and perfect amid the towering pines that surrounded it. The way the waters of Lake Michigan, shimmering just a stone's throw away, beckoned. The cozy feeling of the cedar logs that formed the walls, and the high, natural wood beams framing skylights that allowed light to stream in even on the grayest of days. Though it was small, with just a single bedroom, a great room and galley kitchen, it was more than enough space for her. She'd turned the upper loft into her studio where she could happily lose herself in her work, when the weather wouldn't permit her to paint outside. Despite the unreliable

Michigan weather and its often turbulent storms, Sidney much preferred to paint in the open air, by the water's edge, rather than paint her subjects from memory. There was just something about the antics of the waterfowl that were her specialty that could always be counted on to make her smile. The ducks, the geese, the herons that fished these waters were natural clowns, causing no end of amusement. Best of all, they seemed undisturbed by her presence. Because they'd become accustomed to her sitting at her easel along the shore, they went about their business without distraction.

With the dog and cat sniffing a hundred scents in the forest, Sidney pulled the loaded wagon along the trail through the woods until she emerged in bright sunlight at the water's edge. This was one of her favorite spots. It took only minutes to set up her equipment. Then, after watching a family of ducks splashing near shore, beside a half-submerged wooden rowboat that had stood along the shore for years, she picked up her brush and began to bring them to life on her canvas.

Adam Morgan sat straight up in bed, ready to bolt, when he came fully awake and realized he'd been in the throes of the recurring nightmare. Rubbing a hand over his face, it took him a moment to gather his thoughts. The doctors had warned him that these terrifying dreams were part of the healing process. Though the wounds to his body were visible, and therefore easier to tend, the ones in his mind were no less serious. There were too many things about the incident that were still lost to his conscious memory. But they were there, locked away in his mind, and when he relaxed in sleep, they rose to the surface, taunting him with bits and pieces of the terror he'd experienced. There was still so much about the accident that he couldn't remember. But he'd been assured by his doctors that it would all come back to him in time.

He slid out of bed and moved slowly across the room. Filling a glass with water, he gulped down two capsules, then leaned on the bathroom sink and waited for the dizziness to pass. He caught a glimpse of himself in the mirror and winced. Eyes bloodshot. Cheeks and chin darkened by several days' growth of beard. It would take too much energy to shave. Besides, why bother? Who would see him here, in the middle of nowhere?

The doctors had done all they could. Now, they warned him, what he most needed was time. His frown deepened. Time. There would be plenty of that now. He couldn't return to work until the madman who dogged his trail was captured and put away for good. Twice Adam had managed to elude his stalker, and twice the man had proved just as adept at escaping the authorities, despite their best efforts.

It had been Phil Larken, Adam's boss and president of WNN, World News Network, who had arranged for Adam to use this lighthouse as his own private retreat. Though the nearby town of Devil's Cove was small, there was a modern medical clinic and an excellent physical therapist. Since Adam couldn't return to work until he had a clean bill of health from the doctors, and since they weren't about to let him off the hook until he'd completed at least six months of therapy for the shoulder that had been shattered in the blast, this place afforded him the perfect refuge until he could take back his life.

Odd, he thought as he returned to the bedroom. He'd been working nonstop since his college days. He couldn't remember the last time he'd taken time off. As a photojournalist for World News Network, he'd covered every hot spot in the world. Asia, Africa, Europe, the Middle East. How ironic that his injuries had occurred not in some troubled corner of the world, but right here in the United States, in New York City, outside the United Nations Building.

Now, here he was, feeling as though he'd been caught in a time warp. He looked around as though still doubting he was really here. The last time he'd been in Devil's Cove, he'd been all of twelve, on a fishing trip with his uncle. He'd taken one look at the lighthouse that sat on a finger of land that jutted into Lake Michigan and fell wildly, madly in love.

There was just something about the look of it. That tall spire looking out over miles and miles of nothing but dark water, its beacon the only warning the captain and crew of ships plying this lake had of the dangerous shoals and shallows that lurked beneath the waves.

And now it was his home. At least until he healed. And all because, in a moment of dark depression, he'd confided in Phil that if he had to do nothing for six months, he'd surely go crazy. When Phil asked if there was any place he might be able to endure the boredom, Adam had blurted out his boyhood fascination with the lighthouse. The next thing he knew, Phil had used his considerable influence to make it happen. Adam had been invited by the historical society to spend the off-season living in the Devil's Cove lighthouse, in exchange for photographing the various changes of season for their almanac. Simple work. A simple lifestyle. And because it had all been arranged quickly, and in complete privacy, the authorities were hoping that this time, his stalker would be confounded. Not that Adam believed it was over and he was safe. He'd believe that only when the assassin who'd triggered the car bomb that killed the ambassador and his assistant was behind bars, and not a minute sooner.

Moving like a slug he climbed the dozens of stairs that led to the tower. Though the ships passing through the Great Lakes had long ago switched to

the latest in high-tech navigational equipment, and
the lighthouse was no longer necessary to the boat-
ers' safety, the computer-operated light still went on
every day at dusk and stayed on until morning.
There was something comforting in that. The same-
ness of it gave him a sense that, in a world gone
crazy, some things never changed.

When he reached the top he looked down at the
serene waters, reflecting the forest that ringed its
banks, alive with fiery autumn foliage. Smoke
drifted from an ore carrier moving slowly upriver.
In the distance was a ship bearing a foreign flag.
Several sailboats danced across the waves, and
Adam wondered at the hardy souls willing to risk
the wrath of frigid water and fickle winds. Still, if
he had the strength, he knew he'd be out there with
them. Hadn't he always enjoyed a challenge? It was
one of the reasons he thrived on the dangers of his
job.

He walked over to the telescope he'd set up, so
that he could keep a close eye on his surroundings.
He peered through the lens, thinking there couldn't
be a more beautiful place in the world than Michigan in fall. Especially here on the shore of Lake
Michigan. As long as he had to spend his sick leave
somewhere private, there wasn't anywhere he could
think of that would suit him more, so long as he
could see an end to the idyll. He knew himself well
enough to be certain that even paradise would seem

like a prison to him if it stretched on endlessly. He was determined to get out of here as soon as the doctor's projected goal of six months of therapy was over. He shook his head, trying to recall the last time he'd spent six months in one place.

Now that the daylight was fading to dusk, he decided to grab a camera and try for a few shots of the nearby forest at sunset. If nothing else, it would take his mind off his pain and boredom.

Sidney alternately watched the antics of the duck family and lowered her head to return her attention to her canvas, perfectly capturing the line, the form, the symmetry of each of her models.

In early spring she'd watched this pair of proud mallards bring their six babies to the water and hover over them as they'd taken their first swim near shore. Now the six were as big as their parents, and ready for the flight south with other migrating flocks. To prepare for the grueling trip, they were driven to search out as much food as their bodies could hold. Tipping upside down to feed on the bottom of the shallows, only their tail feathers were visible. It was a sight she always found endearing. She'd already thought of the title for the painting. Bottom's Up. That had her grinning.

Though the earlier afternoon sunshine had caused her to discard her corduroy jacket and roll her sleeves, she now shivered in the gathering shadows as she struggled to put this entire scene on canvas before the duck family decided to depart for warmer climates.

Picasso lay at her feet, panting from his romp in the woods, his fur matted with burrs that would take most of the evening to remove. Toulouse was no-where to be seen, but Sidney wasn't worried. Even if he stayed out all day stalking field mice, that cat was smart enough to show up at her door in time for dinner. Toulouse never missed a meal or a chance to curl up before the fire.

She added a dab of paint to her palette, mixed it and bent to her work.

Picasso's ears lifted. He sprang to his feet, a low warning growl issuing from his throat.

Surprised, Sidney turned in time to see a shadow emerging from the cover of the woods. As the shadow separated itself from the others, she realized it was a man. At first, judging by his rough beard and even rougher garb, she thought he might be a hunter, until she realized that he was carrying, not a rifle, but a camera. A second camera hung from a strap around his neck.

He paused, allowing the dog to get close enough to take his scent.

"Sorry. Didn't mean to startle you." His voice was deep, the words spoken abruptly, as though he resented having to speak at all.

Sidney set aside her brush and wiped her hands

on a rag before getting to her feet. "We don't see too many people out here."

"I didn't expect to run into anybody." He glanced around. "I don't see a car or a boat. How'd you get here?"

"I live over there." She pointed to the forest at his back.

"In those woods?" He shot her a look of surprise. "I was told this was federally protected land."

"It is. Or at least most of it is. My property was grandfathered in before the government bought the surrounding land. It's been owned by the same family since the turn of the century, so it remained private property. When it went on the market, I liked the idea of a guarantee that there would never be any neighbors."

She could feel him studying her a little too intensely. When an uncomfortable silence stretched between them she tried a smile. "How about you? I don't believe I've seen you around Devil's Cove before."

He didn't return the smile. "Just moved in." He watched the way the dog moved to stand protectively beside Sidney. "I'm staying in the lighthouse."

"Really?" She turned to study the tower that could be seen above the tree line. "How did you manage that? I thought it was an historic building now, and off-limits to the public."

"Just lucky, I guess. The historical society asked me to photograph the area for their almanac. In exchange, I get to stay there until next spring."

"Then you're a professional photographer?"

"Yeah." He glanced at the canvas. "And from the look of that, I'd guess I'm in the company of a professional artist."

When he made no move to introduce himself, Sidney offered her hand. "I'm Sidney Brennan."

He seemed to pause a beat before saying gruffly, "I think I've seen some of your work. Wildlife?"

She nodded.

"Adam Morgan."

He had a strong, firm handshake, she noted. And his eyes stayed steady on hers until she withdrew her hand and motioned toward the dog at her feet. "This is Picasso."

When he looked down, the dog cocked his head to one side and regarded him. "A good watchdog."

She laughed. "He knows who feeds him."

"Lucky dog. Since I have to feed myself, I'm about to head back and see about dinner."

"Dinner?" Sidney glanced up at the sky, noting for the first time that the sun had begun to slip below the horizon. "I had no idea it was so late."

"That must mean you were having a good day."

She nodded, surprised that he understood. "That's right. I get so lost in my work, I forget everything. I even forget to eat."

"Yeah. I know the feeling." He turned toward the lighthouse in the distance. "Good night."

"Nice to meet you, Adam. Maybe I'll see you again some time." Sidney began to pack up her paints.

Seeing her fold up her easel and camp stool to pack them in the wagon, he paused, taking her measure. She was no bigger than a minnow and couldn't weigh a hundred pounds. "You sure you can handle all that?"

"Don't worry. I haul it all the time."

She'd gone only a few paces when he fell into step beside her.

At her arched eyebrow he merely took the handle from her hands. "Sorry. I've forgotten my manners. Living alone does that. I'd feel a lot better if you'd let me pull this."

It was on the tip of her tongue to refuse. She didn't know this man, and wasn't sure she wanted to get to know him. But she was feeling the effects of working all day without eating. Not really weak so much as light-headed. The thought of having help hauling this equipment home was comforting. "Thanks."

As they followed the path deeper into the woods, Sidney looked up at the canopy of fiery autumn foliage. "You picked a great time of year to visit."

When he didn't reply, she added, "This is my favorite season."

"For the color?"

"There's that, of course. But it's more. The tourists are gone, a lot of the trendy shops are closed until next summer, and there's this wonderful feeling of anticipation."

He turned to her. "What is it you're anticipating?"

She shrugged. "Slowing down, I guess. Settling in for the winter. Have you ever spent a winter in Michigan?"

"No. Tell me what I'm in for."

She laughed. "Snow. Mountains of it. I hope you like skiing, sledding and ice fishing."

"I'll let you know after I've tried my hand at all of them."

"Where are you from?"

Again that pause, as though reluctant to reveal anything about himself. "Florida, originally. But it's been years since I've been back."

"Where do you live when you're not here photographing nature?"

"Wherever an assignment takes me."

"Assignment?"

"I'm a photojournalist with WNN."

Her eyes widened. "Really? I've never met anyone who actually worked for television news before. I suppose you've been all over the world."

He merely gave a shrug of his shoulders, as though reluctant to talk about his work. And though it was on the tip of her tongue to ask why he was here in Devil's Cove, instead of some exotic location, there was something about his closed, shuttered look that told her he wouldn't be comfortable answering any more of her questions.

They came up over a rise and Adam stopped dead in his tracks at the sight of the cabin. "Talk about isolation."

Sidney couldn't decide if he was impressed or dismayed. "I guess I'm just comfortable with my own company. I knew the minute I saw it that it had to be mine."

He shot her a sideways glance as she opened the door and held it while he stepped past her. Once inside he handed her the easel and stool, and she set them in a corner of the room, along with her paints and canvas.

When she turned, she saw him rubbing his shoulder. "Are you all right?"

"Yeah." He lowered his hand. "Just nursing an injury."

"You should have told me."

He shook his head. "Nothing to worry about. I'm fine."

Sensing that he was uncomfortable talking about it, she quickly changed the subject. "How about some cider before you go?"

"Cider?"

"Don't tell me you've never tried our Michigan

cider?'' Sidney opened the refrigerator and removed
a jug. ''Apple cider. Made just outside of town at
the Devil's Cove Orchard and Old Mill.'' She nodded toward the great room. ''Make yourself comfortable. I'll bring you a mug. You're in for a treat.''

''I'll stay here.'' He remained by the door. ''My
boots would track dirt on your floor.''

''You could take them off.''

''I'd rather not.''

When he didn't move, Sidney filled two mugs
with cider and handed him one before crossing to
the fireplace, where she held a match to kindling.
Within minutes a cozy fire was burning on the
hearth.

She looked at the window with a laugh. ''I see
Toulouse is back.''

While Adam watched with interest, she walked
over, reached around him and opened the door. The
black-and-white cat bounded inside and crossed the
room to settle on a rug in front of the fire, where he
began grooming himself.

''Another one of yours?'' Adam asked.

She nodded. ''Toulouse found us about six
months ago. Just wandered in and never left.''

''Smart cat.'' Adam sipped his cider and looked
around the cozy cabin, letting the warmth of the fire
soothe his aching shoulder. The place smelled of
cedar, apples and faintly of linseed oil. A bowl of
apples adorned the coffee table set in front of the

sofa. He looked up, admiring the rugged cedar beams overhead. Spying the loft he tilted his head for a better look. ''Your studio?''

''Yes. It's perfect under the skylights. I usually work there only when I can't paint outside. But I much prefer working in the fresh air, with my models posing in the water close to shore.''

''Models?''

She laughed. ''Ducks. Geese. All kinds of waterfowl. They're my specialty.''

''I see.'' He noted the number of canvases, stacked in no apparent order along the wooden railing, and the easel positioned directly under the skylights. ''I guess I'll need some models, too. Deer and foxes, and whatever else I can scare up in these woods.''

''You'll be amazed at how much wildlife you'll see. This forest is alive with some wonderful creatures.''

He heard the warmth in her tone. ''I'm counting on it. I'm hoping to put together a workable darkroom at the lighthouse, so I won't have to send my work to an outside lab. There's a fairly good-size utility room on the lower level that I think might work. It has a small sink and several long cabinets connected by a countertop. I think it'll give me the room I need to develop my prints.''

It was, Sidney realized, the most he'd said since they'd met. ''It's so nice to be able to work at home.

If you're like me, you're going to like living and working in the same space.'' She settled herself on the raised hearth and absently ran a hand over Toulouse's back. The cat closed his eyes and purred contentedly.

''Yeah, there's something to be said for that.'' Adam found himself watching the cat with envy. Sometimes when Marcella Trowbridge, his physical therapist, whom he'd silently dubbed The Dominatrix, was pushing him to the limits of endurance, he wanted to ask her to stop and just massage his shoulder instead. Of course, Marcella wasn't being paid to soothe him. Her job was to get him back to normal, or as close to normal as possible, in the shortest amount of time. And she did that by beating him up on a regular basis, until he wanted to beg for mercy. Each time their therapy session ended, he felt like a whipped dog. He was intelligent enough to know it was necessary, and that it was, indeed, getting the job done. Without the therapy, he'd never be allowed back to work. But he couldn't help wishing for it to be over sooner rather than later.

To keep from thinking about what it would be like to be the one getting a back rub, he turned his attention to the rest of the room. The walls were hung with paintings of waterfowl. Some were sweet. Families of ducks or geese swimming in perfect formation, mother in front, young in the middle, the father taking up the rear, head lifted to guard against predators. Some were poignant, like the one of a pair of ducks anxiously guiding their lone baby into the water for a first swim.

He stepped closer, careful to keep his muddy boots on the small square of rug at the door. "Those are wonderful. Are you able to make a living with your art?"

Sidney nodded. "I consider myself lucky. Several galleries carry my work. And since my sister Courtney came back to Devil's Cove and opened her shop, I haven't been able to keep up with the demand." She laughed. "My grandfather likes to say that Courtney could sell sand in the desert."

"I know the kind. A real people person. But I'm betting she doesn't have to twist any arms to sell this. You have an amazing talent."

"Thank you." She heard the wind pick up outside and glanced at the window where red-and-gold leaves tumbled in a wild dance. The air had grown considerably colder now that the sun had set. On impulse she said, "I'm thinking of making an omelette for dinner. Would you like to stay?"

He gave a quick shake of his head and drained his mug before setting it on the kitchen table. "Sorry. I've got to go. But you were right. The cider was great."

"I thought you'd like it."

That wasn't all he liked. If he didn't know better, he'd think he had just stumbled into some sort of enchanted cottage. And the red-haired woman with the soft green eyes was either a witch or a goddess.

He resolutely turned the knob and pulled open the door, absorbing a blast of chilly wind. "Good night."

Sidney hurried across the room and stood in the doorway, the dog and cat at her feet. "Good night, Adam. Maybe I'll see you again sometime."

Not likely, he thought as he started toward the beacon of light in the distance. The last thing he needed was a female cluttering up his already messed-up life. Especially one that smelled of evergreen and had hair the color of autumn leaves, not to mention eyes all soft and deep and green. Eyes that a man could drown in.

He'd already made up his mind to carefully keep his distance from Sidney Brennan.

Chapter 2

Adam carefully looked around the grounds of the lighthouse for signs that anyone had been here while he'd been gone. Confident that nothing had been disturbed, he shoved open the door and set his camera on a nearby table. Since the explosion, and subsequent attempts on his life, extreme caution had become second nature to him.

Not that he'd ever been careless. His work had taken him to some of the most dangerous hot spots in the world. He'd covered wars, revolutions, uprisings and rebellions for WNN. Life in a war zone had taught him many things. Among them, to trust his instincts, to know not only where he was headed, but how to escape a trap. His associates used to boast that he had eyes in the back of his head. How ironic that it had been here at home, with his guard down, that he'd found himself in the greatest peril of his life.

He started toward the kitchen, thinking about the day he'd put in. He'd just spent hours on a trek through the woods, capturing the spirit of northern Michigan in autumn. Though he'd seen deer before, it was different watching them in their natural habitat. They were careful animals, he'd noted. Heads lifted often to catch any strange scent. The buck standing guard while the herd feasted on the tender branches of low-hanging trees. Not so different from people, he realized. Always looking out for any danger that might threaten. By the time they'd finally caught his scent and melted into the forest, he'd used up an entire roll of film.

There had been humor in the forest, as well as beauty. A squirrel, busy storing acorns in the hollow of a giant oak, had been his first model. Then he'd come across a spider spinning a web, intricate as finest lace, damp with dew and glistening in the thin rays of sunlight that filtered through the branches of towering evergreens. Next he'd spotted a flock of geese honking as they flew overhead in perfect formation on the first leg of their southward journey. No sooner had they passed than he'd come upon two chipmunks that performed a comedy routine by leaping into a mound of red-and-gold leaves, then leaping out again with their precious store of nuts puffing out their tiny faces. They'd managed to entertain him for an hour or more.

Odd, he thought, how much vibrant life he'd discovered in these woods. He'd come here expecting to be bored. After a lifetime spent covering wars and terrorist uprisings, recording the range of human emotion from despair to euphoria, from depravity to heroism, he wouldn't have believed he could be amused, entertained and thrilled, all in a matter of hours merely by tramping through a Michigan forest. What's more, he was learning to look at life on a smaller scale rather than the large canvas he'd been using for most of his adult life. When he took the time to look, really look, he'd managed to find beauty, humor and even drama alive and well in the seclusion of the forest.

Idly rubbing his shoulder he heated up the last of the morning's coffee. After two sips he nearly gagged before tossing the rest down the drain and turning away. He promised to treat himself to a fresh cup in town after another therapy session with The Dominatrix.

If he was making any improvement, he couldn't see or feel it. The pain never left him, and the range of movement seemed unchanged since he'd first begun therapy. If it wasn't for the fact that he needed this therapist's signature, as well as his surgeon's, on a set of discharge documents required by WNN, he would simply forego any future torture. Still, Marcella The Dominatrix insisted he was showing definite improvement. And this was, he knew, more than just a chance to heal. It had been singled out as the perfect refuge from an assassin bent on eliminating any witnesses to his crime. The authorities were convinced that no one could penetrate their secrecy and locate their witness in this wilderness.

Adam was hoping they were right. But he wasn't about to let down his guard.

He walked outside, climbed into his Jeep and headed for town.

The afternoon was bathed in sunlight and warm enough to be sultry, but he wasn't fooled. The nights had become increasingly cooler, with a hint of frost. And though the waters of Lake Michigan were placid enough today, he'd seen angry whitecaps whipping the waters into foam that sent a spray hundreds of feet into the air as the surge of water thrashed against the base of the lighthouse.

He followed the narrow trail that led to the highway, until he caught sight of a figure hauling a wagon and moving away from the water's edge, trailed by a dog and cat. Just seeing Sidney had him frowning. He'd worked very hard these last couple of days to avoid going near the area where he'd first seen her sitting at her easel.

The authorities might believe he was safely hidden away here, but he wasn't taking any chances.

He had no right to involve an innocent bystander in the danger and chaos that had become his life.

At some other time, in some other place, it would have been an interesting challenge to get to know the sweet, pretty artist. As usual, the timing was all wrong.

He could certainly keep his distance for six months. After all, he'd managed to keep any serious commitments at bay for years now while he pursued this career that was as demanding as any mistress.

Sidney glanced at the lighthouse towering above the line of trees, before reluctantly heading toward her cabin. She found herself wondering, as she had all week, about the man who was now living there.

His brief visit had been an unexpected treat. Though she enjoyed her solitude and never tired of her own company, there was no denying that she'd been curious about Adam Morgan ever since their meeting.

It had been too long since she'd allowed anyone other than family to invade her privacy. Adam's brief presence hadn't felt like an invasion. He'd been oddly distant, but also quiet and respectful of her work. Being an artist himself, he understood her need for solitude and seemed to share her work ethic. That appealed to her on so many levels. She missed having someone to talk to about her work. Not the technique, which she'd mastered at a very

young age, but the passionate love of the work itself.
There were times, when a painting was finished, that
it felt like pure magic. As though someone else had
taken over her body and mind and soul, and had
created something out of nothing. She had never
been able to explain the feeling of transforming a
blank canvas into color and form and the living,
breathing creatures looking out at her from her
paintings.

With Adam, she hadn't needed to explain. She'd
sensed that he knew exactly what it was she did and
how she did it. What's more, he shared that artist's
eye for the interesting and intriguing.

She shoved a tangle of hair from her eyes and
paused to study the day's work. She'd captured a
pair of old-squaws that had flown into the shallows
several days ago. There was no telling how long
they would stay before continuing their southward
migration. Their color wasn't spectacular. Both male
and female were dull brown and white. But the
male's bill was tinged with bright orange, and his
tail a long wisp that fluttered like a ship's sail in the
breeze. They'd been delightful subjects for her canvas.

When Picasso had decided to cool off in the shallows, the pair of ducks, angry at this intrusion, took
refuge on shore, giving Sidney a chance to see their
feathers at closer range. Working quickly she'd
added depth and texture to the painting. By the time

the dog had returned to lie at her feet, and the ducks were safely back in the water, she'd been lost in her work, and had remained so for hours.

Now it was time to head home. She'd promised her grandparents a visit, and she would use the visit to town to stock up on some supplies, as well. As she followed the familiar trail, she was struck by the beauty of the day. Sunlight filtered through the branches of the trees, casting the ground in light and shadow. The air was so mild she'd been forced to remove her sweater and roll the sleeves of her shirt.

At the cabin she stowed her canvas and equipment, leaving the wagon just outside the door. Then she took the time to feed Picasso and Toulouse. That done, she tucked her shopping list in her backpack, tied the sleeves of her sweater around her waist and headed for the log building out back that served as both storage shed and garage. Because the day was so lovely, she decided to forego the Land Rover in favor of her bike.

As she climbed aboard and began peddling past the cabin, she found herself laughing at the forlorn sight of her dog and cat watching from the window.

"Sorry, babies. Maybe next time."

The dog set up a loud yapping, while the cat turned his back on her, as though giving her the cold shoulder.

That only had her laughing harder. The poor little things had no idea why they were being excluded from this latest adventure. All they knew was that they were being left behind, and were doing their best to let her know how bitterly disappointed they were.

"I'll see you Tuesday. One o'clock all right for you?" Marcella Trowbridge waited, pen poised over her appointment book, while Adam buttoned his shirt.

"That's fine."

"Good." She filled in the time, added it to an appointment card and handed it to him before snapping the book shut.

He tucked his shirt into his jeans and studied the woman who, though no more than five-and-a-half feet tall, had hands strong enough to make him want to whimper in pain every time she touched him. "Seems like everyone in this clinic is a native of Devil's Cove. Are you one of them?"

She shook her head, sending frizzy blond corkscrew curls dancing around a chubby face that was always wreathed in smiles. "I've only been here a couple of months."

"What brought you here?" He probed his shoulder, feeling as if he'd just come through a war.

"Funny story. I had no idea of leaving the big city. But a friend of mine from University Hospital opened her new clinic and I drove up for the open house, without realizing that she had space to lease.

I took one look at this quaint little place and decided I had to give small-town living a try. Within two months I'd given up my apartment in Lansing, found a place to live just a block away from here, overlooking the water and signed a lease on this suite.''

''Can you make a living here?''

She laughed. ''I'll say. Not only does my friend give me plenty of referrals, but my old friends at University Hospital keep sending me more than I can handle.'' Marcella shook her head. ''Strange how these things happen. I'm working more hours than ever, and yet I'm letting go of all the stress I once had working in a big city. I recently went through a painful divorce, vowed I'd never put myself through the marriage game again, and now I'm engaged to the pharmacist who works in suite Twelve-A. Go figure. And all because of my friendship with Dr. Emily Brennan-Cooper.''

Adam's hand paused in the act of turning the door handle. ''Brennan-Cooper? Does she have a sister named Sidney?''

''Yeah. The artist. You know her?''

''We met. She mentioned a sister who owned a gift shop. I didn't realize there were more.''

''I can see that you're not spending enough time in town. Everywhere you turn, you'll find a Brennan. Let's see.'' She thought a minute. ''Far as I know, she has a mother, three sisters, prominent grandparents. Her grandmother was a teacher here for thirty or forty years. Her grandfather is retired Judge Frank Brennan. Her father was the town doctor before he died, and now my pal Emily has stepped in and taken over his practice. Besides which, the pretty doc is married to Jason Cooper.''

''The bestselling author?''

''Yep.'' Marcella's smile grew. ''Her mother owns her own real-estate firm and handles most of the mansions over on Historic Scenic Drive. Her sister Hannah owns Hannah's Garden and Landscape, and her sister Courtney is the one who owns Treasures, a fancy gift shop in town.'' She paused a beat, as though considering how to ask a delicate question, before deciding to simply plow ahead. ''How did you happen to settle on Devil's Cove?''

He merely shrugged. ''One place is as good as another when it's just a temporary port, Marcella. Thanks.'' He winced as he touched his shoulder. ''I think.''

She was staring after him with a puzzled grin as he pulled the door shut. He was certainly living up to his reputation as the town's new mystery man. Though he'd managed to find out all about her within a minute or so, she knew no more about him now than when he'd arrived for his first session.

She gave a toss of her curls. ''Sooner or later I'll find out about you, Adam Morgan.''

She loved a good mystery.

* * *

Adam handed his prescription refill to the girl behind the counter. He was mulling over the shelves of pain relievers, wondering if he needed something for sleep, when he caught the sudden flash of red hair peddling past his line of vision.

Curious, he moved to the window of the drugstore and watched as Sidney propped her bicycle against the wall of the building across the street and walked inside.

He couldn't help admiring the view of her backside in slim, snug denims before she disappeared through the doorway.

A short time later, noting which way Sidney was going, he tucked his prescription into his pocket and headed in the opposite direction, toward The Pier, which had come highly recommended.

If he felt a twinge of guilt at his deliberate attempt to ignore her, he pushed it aside. After all, it was for her own good.

"Sidney." Her grandmother stood framed in the doorway as Sidney lowered the kickstand of her bike and raced up the front steps of the Willows.

"Hi, Bert." Sidney gave her grandmother a warm hug before stepping past her. "Mmm. Something smells wonderful."

"Trudy is baking pies."

"What's the occasion?"

"No special reason. She just said she always feels like baking pies in the fall."

"I'm sure Poppie will be happy to eat them."

The older woman winced. "That's what I'm afraid of. Which is why you'll have to take a few home with you."

"I'll take one. That's all the room I can manage with my bike's basket."

"If I had my way you'd take all of them."

They walked arm in arm along the cool tiled hallway. When they stepped into the cozy, sun-drenched kitchen, Sidney was surprised to see her sisters Hannah and Emily at the table, enjoying slices of freshly baked pie and steaming cups of tea.

"I didn't know you'd be here." With a laugh Sidney danced across the floor to hug each of her sisters. "Where's Courtney?"

"At her shop. She said she'd be by later to enjoy some of Trudy's pie."

The housekeeper looked up from the stove. Her white hair, damp from the heat of the oven, was curled like cotton balls around a face that crinkled into a smile at the sight of another of her girls. "Don't you look fresh." She gave Sidney an approving glance before accepting a kiss on the cheek. "Living out in the wilderness seems to agree with you."

"It's not exactly the wilderness, Trudy." Sidney accepted a slice of pie on a crystal plate and settled herself at the table beside her grandmother. "I've got electricity, heat, light and even the Internet. What more could a girl ask?"

"Neighbors," the housekeeper said in her trademark raspy voice. "Your family would feel a whole lot better if you could count on someone nearby in times of trouble."

Sidney glanced around the table. "It just so happens I do have a neighbor."

Hannah's head came up. "The mystery man in the lighthouse?"

Sidney seemed puzzled. "You've heard of him?"

"Only that someone's living there. Have you actually met him?"

At Sidney's quick nod, her two sisters looked intrigued.

Hannah's pie was forgotten. "What's his name?"

"Adam Morgan."

Emily took a sip of tea. "What does he look like?"

Sidney shrugged. "Tall. Rugged. It's hard to tell what he'd look like without that beard."

Hannah grinned. "He has a beard?"

"He does. And hair that really needs a trim. It brushes his collar."

"Dark hair or light?" Hannah demanded.

"Dark. Like his eyes." Sidney's voice lowered. "His eyes are...I don't know. Penetrating, I guess.

He has a way of looking at me that makes me uncomfortable.''

"In what way?'' Alarmed, Trudy picked up a wooden spoon and held it in a threatening gesture.

"Not in a bad way, Trudy. He just seems intense. As though trying to read my mind while guarding his own.''

"A mystery man.'' Hannah sighed. "There's nothing quite like an air of mystery to get a girl's interest.''

"I'm not interested.'' Sidney looked around the table at the sly grins being exchanged between her sisters. "He's abrupt and distant, and besides, I've only seen him once, and that was more than a week ago.''

"What was more than a week ago?'' At the booming voice of her grandfather, Sidney pushed away from the table.

"Poppie.'' She wrapped her arms around his neck and kissed him on his cheek. "Oh, I've missed you.''

"I've missed you, too, my darling. When are you going to move back home?''

"Sorry. I've left you for good. I'm having way too much fun in my own place.''

He chose to ignore that. "I see Bert and Trudy conspired to have you join your sisters in eating as much pie as possible, in order to save me from indulging in too many calories.''

"Guilty." Sidney joined in the laughter.

"Now tell me what happened more than a week ago?"

Before Sidney could answer, Hannah said, "She met the mystery man who's living in the lighthouse."

"And is he a werewolf, as some in town have claimed?"

At Sidney's puzzled look he threw back his head and roared. "You can't believe all the rumors floating around about the man. That he only comes out after dark. That he's in the Federal Witness Protection Plan, and is starting a new life. That he's a former CIA agent hoping to write a book. So..." The Judge helped himself to a bite of Sidney's pie before releasing the fork when he caught a threatening look from his wife. "What do you know about the man?"

"His name is Adam Morgan. He's a photographer with World News Network, and he's living in the lighthouse while he assembles some photographs for the historical society's almanac."

Hannah turned to their grandmother. "You're a member of the historical society, Bert. Why didn't you tell us?"

The older woman shrugged. "It was all handled very discreetly. We were told only that the man in question came highly recommended by his em-

ployer, that he won a Pulitzer for one of his war
photographs..."

"He won a Pulitzer?" Sidney's eyes went wide.
"Are you sure?"

Bert nodded. "As I said, he came highly recommended. We wouldn't allow just anyone to live in
one of our historic treasures."

"A prize-winning photographer." The Judge
poured himself a cup of tea. "Living practically next
door to our Sidney." He sipped and glanced around
the table with that impish grin they had all come to
recognize. "Now, isn't that interesting?"

Sidney could feel her cheeks coloring as she de-
posited her plate and cup in the dishwasher. "I need
to get back before dark."

"I could drive you," Emily offered. "I have a
couple of evening appointments at the clinic."

"It's too far out of your way. I can manage."

As Sidney started toward the door, Trudy stopped
her with a pie, neatly wrapped in foil.

"Thanks, Trudy." She kissed the housekeeper's
cheek, then circled the table kissing her family
goodbye. "See you at Sunday brunch."

Hannah's eyes twinkled with teasing laughter. "If
you happen to run into that mystery man, you could
always entice him into your cabin with Trudy's
pie."

While the others laughed, the Judge huffed out a

breath. "As if any of the Brennan women need pie to snag a man's interest."

"Good one, Poppie. I can always count on you to stand up for me." Laughing along with the others, Sidney blew her grandfather a kiss before walking out the door.

Chapter 3

Sidney waved at old friends and neighbors as she pedaled her bike through the dusk-shadowed streets of town. Once she'd left Devil's Cove behind, she found herself deep in thought over what little she'd learned about Adam Morgan.

Her mystery man wasn't just a photojournalist, but an award-winning one, as well. Not that she was too surprised. There was an intensity about him that suggested that whatever he attempted, he would do well.

She'd always admired that in a man. Hadn't it been what had first attracted her to Curt? She'd fallen in love with his work before ever meeting him.

It pleased her to know that she could think of Curt now without tears. At first, every time she spoke his name, or saw a flash of his face in her memory, she'd been battered by grief. Now, each year that passed made the loss more tolerable. She would always love him. He'd been her first love, and the bond between them had been so special, so tender, she knew nothing would ever erase those happy memories from her mind. But she'd moved on. It had helped to come back to Devil's Cove. She'd needed family and friends around her, and the comfort of familiar childhood haunts. It had helped, too, to carve out her own space. Her own life, apart from Curt's. Apart even from that of her own very talented, very driven family.

There had been a few men since Curt, but none who merited more than a passing interest. She knew her family watched and waited, clucking like hens over the fact that she was still alone, but the fact was she liked her life as it was. She had her career. She had Picasso and Toulouse for company. And she had her dreams. Maybe that wasn't enough for some, but it was certainly enough for her. For now.

At a gust of icy wind Sidney ducked her head and pulled up the collar of her jacket. Legs pumping, she began to pedal faster, suddenly eager for the warmth of her cabin. She should have started home sooner, before the sun had disappeared behind the clouds, leaving the gathering darkness and its attendant chill nipping at her heels like the hounds of winter.

Adam cranked up the volume on Bruce Springsteen and turned the Jeep off the highway and onto the dirt road that snaked through the forest. The Lake Michigan perch and the cheesecake at The Pier were as good as promised, and he was feeling mellow, despite the curious stares he'd had to endure from the locals while he ate.

That was the trouble with a small town, he thought. Every new face was a source of speculation. Still, it could work to his advantage, as well. Another new face would spark just as much interest, and would have the authorities moving quickly to investigate. The team assigned to the car bombing was already on high alert to his new location, and had promised to move in at the first sign that security had been breached.

To keep his visits into town to a minimum, he'd loaded up with supplies from the grocery store. His backseat was piled high with bags and boxes. He'd stocked up on film, as well, and was determined to get a darkroom equipped as quickly as possible. That would cut down on his visits to Devil's Cove even more.

He was actually looking forward to living the life of a recluse for the winter. It would be a new experience for him. The very nature of his business made it necessary to move easily in crowds of people. One of the first things he'd mastered was the ability to blend in. Whether he was photographing soldiers at war, children in a jungle clearing, or women haggling at an open-air market, he made certain that no one took any notice of him. That was what gave him the opportunity to move freely among strangers, snapping pictures without making his subjects appear self-conscious. No matter where he was, no matter the faces of those around him, Adam had the uncanny ability to become one of them.

He was thinking about the children he'd met at an orphanage in Afghanistan as he rounded a curve in the road. For an instant there was a flash of color that barely registered in his brain as he hit the brakes with such force, the Jeep fishtailed and turned a full circle. The dirt spewing from his wheels rose up in a cloud of dust that obliterated everything. Before the vehicle had even come to a stop he hit the door and scrambled out, struggling to see through the curtain of dust to where Sidney was lying in a tangle of bike and arms and legs.

Nerves had him swearing viciously as he dropped to his knees. "Don't move. Don't you even think of moving. Where does it hurt?" His voice was gruff with self-loathing. "Sorry. I was going too fast. I never even saw you."

"I'm...okay." Sidney started to sit up and was startled when his hands closed roughly over her upper arms.

"I told you not to move." His face was thrust nose-to-nose with hers. His hot breath stung her cheek. "Something could be broken."

"I think I'd know if I'd broken any bones." She tried to evade his touch, gingerly lifting a hand to her head. "I'm just a bit dizzy."

"Hold still. It might be a concussion."

She shook her head and waited until his face came into sharper focus. "I think I just had the wind knocked out of me."

She saw him take in a long, deep breath. All the while his eyes never left hers. "You're sure? You're not bleeding? Nothing's broken?"

"Not as far as I can tell."

"Think you can stand?"

She nodded and he wrapped his arms around her, helping her gently to her feet. In that instant she felt a rush of heat so intense, she could do nothing more than stand quietly, sucking in several deep breaths.

"Any dizziness?"

"I'm..." She struggled to find her voice. "I'm fine."

"I'm driving you home."

She started to turn back. "My bike..."

"I'll put it in the back of my Jeep." He walked with her to his car and held the passenger door open,

practically lifting her off her feet until she was settled inside.

After stowing her bike in the back, he climbed
into the driver's side.

He turned to study her and she felt again that
quick sizzle of heat along her spine. "You okay?"

She nodded, afraid to trust her voice.

They drove the entire distance in silence. When
he pulled up to her cabin, he turned off the ignition
and turned to her. "I'm really sorry about this."

"No harm done."

"You may think so now. By tomorrow you'll be
cussing me out. A spill that hard, I doubt you'll get
away without a few cuts and scratches."

She managed a weak smile. "Nothing I won't
survive."

He walked around and held the door open, then
eased her out of the Jeep and put an arm around her
shoulders as she walked toward the cabin. This time,
though she steeled herself against feeling anything
at his touch, she couldn't deny the reaction. Despite
the cold she was sweating.

The minute she unlocked the door, Picasso and
Toulouse raced out and began dancing around her
feet.

"They act like they just got set free from prison."

She managed a quick laugh. "That's probably
what they're thinking. They whine every time
they're left alone."

Adam paused by the door. ''Where do you store your bike?''

''In the shed in back.'' She handed him her keys.

He returned to the Jeep and lifted her bike out, examining it for damage before heading toward the shed. Minutes later he found her kneeling in front of the fireplace, struggling to coax a fire on the hearth.

Crossing the room he handed her the keys. ''Your bike doesn't seem any the worse for wear. But if you should find any damage, I'd like to pay for it.''

She looked up at him, and for the first time he noticed the bruise beginning to bloom on her cheek.

He swore again, causing her to arch an eyebrow in surprise. ''Sorry.'' He put his hands under her elbows and nearly lifted her off her feet as he propelled her toward an overstuffed chair. ''Sit here. I'll see to the fire.''

''What's wrong?''

He touched a finger to the spot. Just a touch, but he saw her wince in pain. ''You didn't get as lucky as you'd hoped. That's a nasty bruise.''

She lifted her hand and probed. ''I don't remember hitting the ground. But I may have bumped the handlebars. Or maybe a rock on the ground.''

''Whatever you hit, if it moves up just a little, you're going to have a dandy shiner by morning.'' Feeling another round of guilt, he tended to the fire.

When it was blazing, he made his way to the kitchen and put the kettle on the stove.

A short time later he handed her a cup of tea. "Drink this."

"Thanks." She sipped. "Did you make one for yourself?"

"I don't deserve one." Besides, what he really wanted right about now was a good stiff drink. "Got any whiskey?"

"Sorry, no. But there's some wine in the cupboard." Seeing him hesitate, she added, "If you'd like to open the bottle, I'll have some."

"Right." He rummaged around and found the wine and a corkscrew, and filled two glasses.

After handing her one, he perched on the edge of the hearth and studied her pale face. "You sure you're all right?"

She nodded. "I'm fine. Really." She paused. "Did you happen to find a pumpkin pie in the basket of my bike?"

He shook his head. "The basket was empty."

She sighed. "I guess that means the raccoons will feast on Trudy's pumpkin pie tonight."

He started to stand. "I could go back and look for it."

"Leave it, Adam. I'm sure it's nothing but a soggy mess by now, anyway."

Adam frowned as another layer of guilt rolled over him. "Would you like something to eat?"

"No thanks. I couldn't eat a thing."

Feeling suddenly weary, Sidney set her glass beside her cup on the end table and leaned back, closing her eyes. "I think I'll just clean up now and get ready for bed."

He knew she was politely asking him to leave. But guilt held him back. "Maybe I should stay."

She gave him a weak smile. "What could you possibly do that I can't do for myself?"

"Wake you through the night and see if you can focus your eyes. If you can't, I'll know you've suffered a concussion and I can call a doctor."

"That's very kind of you. But my sister Emily is a doctor, and if I'm suffering any ill effects in the morning, I'll be sure to call her." She got slowly to her feet and stood a moment, waiting until the room stopped spinning.

Seeing the way she was holding on to the back of her chair, Adam took a step toward her.

She lifted a hand to stop him. She didn't think she could bear another round of the weakness his touch seemed to cause. "Please. I'm fine now."

"You don't look fine. You look…" Like a piece of fragile crystal, he thought miserably. Or like a tiny bird, its wing broken, hopping just out of reach, refusing to allow itself to be caught by the very one who could most help.

She misread his silence. "I'm sure I'll look much

better after I've had a shower. Now if you'll excuse me.''

Hearing the edge to her tone, he set aside his empty glass and wrote on a slip of paper before passing it to her. ''This is the number of my cell phone. It's always with me. If you should need me for any reason tonight, just call.''

He crossed to the door. When he opened it, the dog and cat came bounding inside, breathless from their run.

When he turned Sidney was standing behind him. While the animals danced around her legs, she held firmly to the door, afraid that if she let go, she'd slide like a spineless jellyfish to the floor.

Seeing the effort she was making to appear normal, Adam decided to take the same route. ''I hope you won't mind if I call you in the morning to see how you're feeling.''

She lifted her head, her chin jutting in defiance. ''Call if you'd like. But it's really not necessary.''

''Then if not for you, I'll do it for myself. Just to be sure that you're all right.''

''Do whatever you please.''

Temper flared. It was bad enough that it had been his carelessness that had caused the accident. Now she was adding fuel to the fire by assuming this air of indifference. Was she doing it just to taunt him?

''If I were free to do as I pleased, I'd…'' Without

being aware of it, his gaze lowered to her mouth, and Sidney felt as if his lips had just branded hers.

For the space of a heartbeat, tension sizzled between them. Neither of them moved. Neither spoke. The very silence seemed to crackle with electricity.

Cold wind swirled around the doorway and down the chimney, sending flames dancing in the fireplace. It wasn't enough to cool the blaze of emotions simmering between them.

When he felt in control once more, Adam spoke in what he hoped was a careful, reasonable tone. "I'm the reason you were hurt, and I just don't want to learn later that I didn't do all that I should have to see to your safety."

"I appreciate that. Really. You've been more than kind." She was already closing the door.

His reaction was automatic, stopping it with the toe of his boot. His voice lowered, a sure sign the temper was simmering, banked very carefully just below the surface. "You have my number. Use it in an emergency."

She gave a slight nod of her head.

"I'm calling you first thing in the morning."

"If you feel the need to. Good night, Adam."

He turned away and stalked to the Jeep. When he looked toward the cabin door it was already closed.

On the drive back to the lighthouse, he unleashed a string of rich, ripe oaths, all directed at his careless driving. If he had been the cause of anything serious, he'd never forgive himself.

Of course, if Sidney Brennan had had the good sense not to be riding a bicycle in the middle of the road, when it was too dark to see her, none of this would have happened. Didn't she have to bear some of the responsibility for this accident, as well?

By the time he'd walked the perimeter of the land around the lighthouse and had satisfied himself that nobody had intruded in his absence, he stepped inside and set the bolts, his temper in full force.

As he built a fire and poured himself a tumbler of whiskey, he tried to rationalize his unreasonable anger. His carelessness had caused an accident that could have been serious. No wonder he'd flown into a rage. After all, he hadn't yet healed from his own accident, and he was well aware of the kind of pain and suffering a body could be forced to endure because of the actions of another. On top of that, he'd had a rough day at the therapist's. Added to that was the fact that he was feeling more like a stranger in his own country than he ever had in some of the most primitive places in the world. For all those reasons, he'd merely overreacted.

As he lifted the tumbler for another sip, his hand stilled.

"Liar," he said aloud. The sound of his voice seemed to echo off the walls. He fell silent for a moment, then tipped back his head and began to chuckle. "Adam Morgan, you lying son of a..." He shook his head again, getting used to the sound of his voice in the empty room.

There was no point in carrying on the lie. He was mad, all right. Mad because, when he'd helped Sidney Brennan up from her fall, his hands had been trembling. Not just from fear, though his first reaction had been a legitimate fear that she'd been hurt. But after he'd been assured that she was all right, he'd wanted, more than anything, to just hold her. And because he knew he had no right to such feelings, he'd resorted to temper, which was much safer.

He'd phone her in the morning as he'd promised, just to assure himself that she was all right. And then, if it killed him, he'd keep his distance, as he'd originally planned.

All of a sudden, after getting too close to the red-haired, green-eyed angel who lived all alone in the woods, the six-month sentence stretching out before him was beginning to look like an eternity.

Chapter 4

Sidney was wrenched from sleep by the shrill ringing of the telephone. After several attempts to pick it up from the night table with her eyes closed, she was forced to open them, which had her wincing in the glare of sunlight spilling through the windows.

At last she fumbled around and managed to lift the phone to her ear. "Yes. Hello."

"Sidney?" The sound of her voice, still a little breathless from sleep and confusion, brought an image to Adam's mind that had him softening his tone. "I was getting worried. How're you feeling?"

"I don't know." When she recognized Adam on the other end of the line, she was instantly alert. "Fine, I guess. I won't know until I'm awake for a while."

"Sorry." He felt his heartbeat begin to steady. "I knew I was taking a chance on waking you, but I had to know whether or not you'd made it through the night with no problems."

"Thanks for your concern." She shoved hair from her eyes as she sat up. The dog and cat, who'd been sleeping at the foot of her bed, took that as a signal that she was up for the day, and started racing toward the door in anticipation of their morning run.

Adam's voice held a note of alarm. "What's all the noise? Is someone there?"

"Just Picasso and Toulouse, getting ready for another adventure."

"Sorry. I can see that my timing's all wrong today."

Sidney smiled. "I'm a little off schedule myself. I'd better go. If I don't let my two spoiled animals out, they'll go stir-crazy."

When the phone went dead Adam continued to cradle it in his hand while he stared out at the expanse of water. He'd been too agitated to sleep last night. Instead, he'd spent the night working on the changes necessary to turn a utility room into a darkroom. Now that he knew Sidney was fine, he'd have no trouble getting in a few solid hours of sleep.

He made his way to his bedroom and drew the shades, hoping the lack of sunlight would be enough to lull him to sleep.

He'd be a whole lot more comfortable, he thought

with a wicked grimace, if Sidney Brennan was here to give him a back rub.

Adam trudged through the woods. Though he'd spent the better part of the day trying to sleep, the image of Sidney had intruded, causing him no end of discomfort. Though he fully intended to stick to his intention of avoiding her, he needed to see just how bruised she was from that encounter with his Jeep. But just for a moment, he promised himself, and then he would leave her to her work and see to his own.

He paused at the edge of the woods and watched her as she sat at her easel. He itched to capture her on film just this way. The laces of her hiking boots peeking out from the hem of her long denim skirt. A tan corduroy jacket layered over a deep green turtleneck. Wind-tossed hair streaming down her back in a cascade of tangles. Her cheeks as red as apples, and her eyes alive with excitement. Palette and brush in her hands as she focused on the scene unfolding before her.

Without giving a thought to what he was doing, he'd framed her in his viewfinder and snapped a couple of shots.

Sidney sat perfectly still, her canvas forgotten as she watched the blue heron standing on one foot in the shallows. There was something so patient about this creature, as it stared into the water, waiting for the school of fish to move closer. She'd seen a heron stand that way for half an hour or more until the time was just right to make its move.

Catching herself dreaming, she worked quickly to sketch the shape of the bird and capture that graceful stance. Then she began filling in the form. The tucked-back wing. The piercing stare. The almost haughty lift of head.

Something distracted the heron and it turned, staring directly beyond her before unfurling those magnificent wings and lifting into the air. Within seconds it was sailing high above the water until it disappeared from sight.

Sidney turned to see what had disturbed the tranquil scene.

Adam stood several feet away, his camera dangling from a cord around his neck. "Sorry. Didn't mean to scare your model."

"It's happened before. He's a bit skittish."

"Or else he figured the fishing would be better where it isn't so crowded." He stepped closer and took a look at the canvas. "You've nailed him, right down to that plume on his head. I'm betting this isn't the first time he's posed for you."

"He's one of my regulars." As Adam dropped to his knees to pet Picasso and Toulouse, Sidney smiled at the sight of the dog and cat vying over which of them would get the most number of pats from his big hand. Each time he scratched behind the dog's ears, Toulouse would intrude himself between them, so that Adam was forced to run a hand along the cat's back as well.

She hadn't expected to see him today, and yet she'd nurtured a tiny hope that she might be wrong. All the while she'd been working, the tantalizing thought of Adam had been hovering on the edges of her mind.

He didn't look nearly as dark and dangerous as he had on their first encounter. Still, that stubble of beard told her he hadn't taken the time to shave. His hair was still in need of a trim, falling over the collar of his plaid flannel shirt. But now, as he straightened and stepped even closer, Picasso and Toulouse at his heels, there was a softness in his eyes and around his mouth that she hadn't noticed before. It gave just enough softness to that handsome, rugged face to tug at her heart.

A gust of raw wind with just a hint of freezing rain caught her hair, whipping it around her face.

He lifted a hand to sweep it back, then cupped her chin, lifting her face for his inspection. "I was right. You've got yourself a beautiful shiner."

At his touch she was forced to absorb the most amazing rush of heat, and wondered that her bones didn't simply melt. "Good thing I don't have to see anybody but you way out here. At least I don't have to explain how I got this a dozen or more times."

His eyes narrowed on her bright red cheeks. "You're freezing. How long have you been here?"

When he turned the full force of that intense gaze on her she felt a sudden thrill. As though a laser beam had just been aimed at her heart. "I don't know. A few hours, I guess."

He kept his hand there a moment longer, loving the feel of her soft skin against his palm. "How about taking a break?"

"I suppose I could. What did you have in mind?"

"Hot coffee, for one. And maybe some soup to chase away the chill." He helped her fold up the easel and tucked it, along with the stool, in the ever-present wagon. "Come on. We'll go to my place. How long since you've been inside the lighthouse?"

"Years." She moved along beside him, feeling a rush of anticipation. "It's been closed to the public for so long, I was probably in grade school the last time I was there."

"Then it's time I gave you a tour."

With the dog and cat trailing behind, they made their way across the narrow finger of land that jutted out into Lake Michigan and was surrounded on three sides by water.

From the outside, the lower level was a fairly good-size building painted stark white, with red shutters and a red-shingled roof. Rising from the center for a hundred feet or more was the light tower, also white, with a circular railing around the lookout, just below the light dome. The dome, which sat at the very top of the tower, was made entirely of glass, and had served as a beacon for sailors for hundreds of years.

Sidney paused and tipped her head back for a better view. "I've always loved the look of this place."

Adam nodded. "The first time I saw it, I was just a kid. But it was love at first sight."

"Really?" She didn't know why his words should warm her so. "I didn't know you'd ever been here before."

"I never expected to be back. Who'd have thought that years later I'd be living here?" He didn't open the door at once, but instead took his time glancing around carefully before unlocking the door and holding it open. "Welcome to my new home."

When Picasso and Toulouse started to follow she dropped to her knees, prepared to stop them.

"Don't shoo them away, Sidney. They're welcome, too."

She looked up. "Are you sure?"

He nodded. "They need a break from the cold as much as we do."

"All right." The minute she moved aside, the animals hurried past her and began nosing around, eager to explore their new surroundings.

Sidney stepped inside and paused in the middle of the room.

Despite the layers of paint that had been added over the years, it looked much as it had when she'd first seen it as a child. Rough-sawn timbers formed the ceiling and walls. Along one wall was a giant fireplace made of local stone. The mantel was a single slab of granite. While she watched, Adam knelt and coaxed a flame from the glowing embers. Within minutes a log was burning, adding soothing warmth to the room.

"I'll get the coffee started. Or would you rather have hot chocolate? That is," he added, "if I remembered to buy milk yesterday."

She shrugged. "Chocolate, if you have it. Coffee if you don't."

"I'll be right back. Make yourself comfortable."

She did, taking the time to study this place Adam now called home. There was little furniture to speak of. A faded sofa and a wooden rocking chair drawn up close to the fireplace. Over the arm a plaid throw had been carelessly tossed. The hardwood floor was softened by an oval rag rug in shades of russet and brown.

While Picasso and Toulouse started up the stairs, she turned toward the kitchen.

Coffee was already beginning to perk. Adam was removing something from the refrigerator. He turned when he heard her footsteps.

"No milk, so I had to make coffee. If you'd like,

I could heat up this morning's chili. I guarantee it'll warm you.''

''You had chili for breakfast?'' At his nod she laughed. ''Hot and spicy, I hope?''

''That's the only way I know how to make it.''

''Good. That's the way I like it.''

''My kind of woman.'' He filled two bowls and set them in the microwave.

At Sidney's arched eyebrow, he chuckled. ''I know what you're thinking. I'm sure the historical society had to think long and hard about ruining the rustic look of the place with such a modern appliance, but they knew if they wanted a man to survive the winter here, they'd better include a few conveniences.''

''Are you a good cook?''

When the timer sounded he removed the bowls and set a basket of rolls in their place. ''Tolerable when it comes to simple American food. I'm getting really good at Middle Eastern cooking.''

''Why?''

He rummaged in a drawer for flatware. ''I've spent a lot of time there. When I wasn't off on assignment, I passed the time at open-air markets, buying whatever was for sale and asking the locals how to cook it.''

''Were they willing to share their recipes with strangers?''

''More than willing. Everywhere I went, I found

the people warm and friendly and willing to open their homes, especially when they heard I was an American.''

She couldn't hide her surprise.

Before she could ask more he removed the rolls from the microwave and handed the basket to Sidney. ''Let's take these to the other room and thaw out in front of the fire.''

Drawing an old wooden bench in front of the sofa, he set down the bowls of chili and left the room, returning minutes later with a pot of coffee and two mugs.

While he filled their mugs, Sidney sat down, grateful for the warmth of the fire.

''I'm so glad you brought me here. This fire feels so good.''

As she and Adam began to eat she couldn't help sighing. ''Oh, this is wonderful. I didn't even realize how hungry I was, or how cold I was, until this minute.''

''See? Aren't you glad I came along to save you from cold and starvation?''

They shared a laugh as they dug into their steaming chili.

''About these places you've been, Adam.'' She sat back to sip her coffee. ''Can you speak the language?''

''A little. Enough to get by. When I couldn't

make myself understood, there was always the universal language.''

"What's that?''

He shrugged. "A hand gesture. A smile. Usually it was a kid who would pick up on a word or phrase they'd heard the soldiers use.''

"Didn't it hurt to see the children affected by so much war?''

"Sure. But I knew I wasn't there to snap pretty pictures. My job was to find the reality. And more than that, the humanity.'' He fell silent as he shoved aside the empty bowl and picked up his mug, and Sidney worried that she might have upset him by her questions.

A moment later he broke the silence. "They're beautiful, you know. And so touching.''

She arched an eyebrow. "Who?''

"The children. Funny and stoic and scared and brave. Through cruel dictators and revolutionaries and freedom fighters and peacekeepers, what amazes me is that they just keep on being kids.''

"Do you have photos of them?''

He nodded. "Hundreds, I suppose.''

"I'd love to see them.''

His smile returned. "I'd love to show them to you sometime.''

"Great.'' She nodded toward the stairs leading to the upper floors. "Now I think we'd better go in search of Picasso and Toulouse. They've been gone a long time, and since the smell of food didn't bring them running, I can only surmise that they're up to no good."

He got to his feet. "Okay, I'll show you the rest of the place, as long as you promise not to say a word about the mess."

She stood at the same moment and nearly lost her balance when she found herself pinned between the sofa and his body. "My lips are sealed."

He reacted instinctively, closing his hands around her upper arms to keep her from stumbling. "Your lips are…" His eyes narrowed, the look in them changing from fun loving to fierce in the blink of an eye. "…the most provocative I've ever seen."

There was no time to step back as he dragged her into his arms and covered her mouth with his in a heart-stopping kiss. For a moment all she could do was stand perfectly still as he continued kissing her until she found herself fighting for breath.

How had her arms found their way around his neck, drawing him even closer? Was it the scrape of his rough beard that excited her, or the press of his strong hands as they moved along her sides? And that mouth. So firm as it took possession of hers.

Her mind was suddenly wiped clear of all thought as she lost herself in his kiss.

She felt the keen edge of excitement, her heart throbbing in her temples, as his thumbs moved up her sides and over her breasts. It was the merest touch, but her body responded as though a switch had been thrown, spreading warmth and light into a room that had been locked in darkness.

It had been so long since she'd allowed a man to kiss her like this. To touch her like this. She was swept by a tidal wave of needs. Needs that, so long denied, had her actually trembling.

Adam knew he needed to step back from the heat. He could feel it, pouring from her to him and back again. And still he lingered over her lips, wanting to fill himself with the sweet, clean taste of her.

As he took the kiss deeper, there was no hesitation in her. She returned his kisses with a hunger that had his heart going into overdrive. And yet, despite her response, he cautioned himself to slow down. Things were moving too far, too fast. Hadn't he vowed to keep his distance, for her sake? Now here he was, breaking all his own rules. One simple kiss, and he was in over his head and in danger of drowning. Even knowing the danger, all he could think of was taking her. Here. Now.

The thought was so overwhelming, he drove her back against the wall and dug his hands into her hair, kissing her with a thoroughness that had them both struggling for breath. When at last he lifted his head, he was forced to drag air into his starving lungs.

Sidney struggled not to moan aloud when his mouth left hers. She saw him watching her and lowered her head to hide the look of disappointment she was certain he could see in her eyes. It shamed her to know that he'd been the one to step back from this.

Adam stood, cursing himself for his lapse. So much for his intention to keep his distance. All he did was get close to this woman and he turned into some clumsy, lovesick high-school jock hoping to impress her with his macho moves.

After several silent moments he managed to say, "I believe I promised you a tour." Without waiting for her he started up the stairs, still calling himself every kind of fool.

His hand on the balcony rail, he noted, was none too steady. And his heart was still racing like a runaway train.

Dangerous, he thought with a frown. Sidney Brennan deserved better than this. And if he had any honor at all, he had to see that this thing ended now. Before she found herself caught up in something beyond anything she could imagine.

He'd never before had a problem stepping back from a woman when he'd put his mind to it. So why was he having such trouble this time?

Maybe she really was a witch, he thought, living in an enchanted cabin, and she'd cast some sort of spell on him.

If so, he'd better find a potion to get free of it, before he dragged her into something that was way over her head.

Chapter 5

Sidney stood perfectly still, waiting for her blurred vision to focus and the light-headed feeling to pass. She couldn't remember when a man's kiss had affected her like this. She must be more out of practice than she'd thought to allow something as simple as a kiss, a touch, to have her reacting in this manner.

When she saw Adam pause and look back, she resolutely put one foot in front of the other and began to climb. She was painfully aware of the fact that he was hurrying ahead. Did that mean that he was already regretting that kiss?

There had been a fierceness in his gaze that had shaken her to the core. But was it hunger? Or merely self-loathing for giving in to a weakness?

Talk about a weakness. She took a deep calming breath. The thought of allowing old emotions to surface after all this time had her breath hitching. She'd been so careful all these years to keep her feelings, her yearnings under wraps. She'd thought them dead. Embalmed, along with her heart. But here she was, feeling more alive than ever. And all because of the taste of this man. His touch had awakened in her a hunger unlike anything she'd ever known. The thought that he might not share her passion left her feeling confused and completely out of her element.

"Here you are." Adam paused in a doorway on the second floor and bent to ruffle Picasso's fur. "Have you two had a chance to see everything yet?"

As if in answer, Toulouse popped his head out of an open duffel, looking like a cartoon cat before leaping free. Not to be outdone by the dog, the cat hurried over to get his share of petting.

By the time Sidney caught up with them, Adam had stepped across the room, as though needing to keep his distance. "This is my bedroom."

She managed a shaky laugh. "If you say so."

He stared at the litter of bags and suitcases, still unpacked, and rolls of film spilling out of an open duffel, seeing it for the first time through her eyes. "Having seen your neat little cabin, I realize this is more mess than you're used to. That comes from living on the road for so many years. But I promise you, there's a bed somewhere under all that.''

''I see it. At least I think that's a bed. Do you think it's been here since they first built the lighthouse?''

He ran a hand over the ancient metal frame and studied the faded patchwork quilt that had seen better days. ''It looks that way. Probably to preserve the authenticity of the place. But I think the historical society added a new mattress. Either that, or my body is so accustomed to the rusty springs that pass for beds in fleabag hotels that any mattress less than fifty years old feels soft.''

She shot him a mock-serious look. ''You really need to stop sugarcoating that glamorous life you've been leading.''

''Yeah. To be perfectly honest, there aren't too many people lining up for my old job. Come on.'' He turned away. ''I'll take you up to the tower.''

With Picasso and Toulouse following, they made their way up the staircase to the lookout.

Adam paused at the doorway that led to the outdoor walkway that ringed the tower, just below the dome. ''I'm afraid the wind is too strong to go out there now, but take my word for it, the view is breathtaking.'' He pointed. ''Let's head on up to the top.''

The circular dome was made almost entirely of glass. From any angle in the room, they could see for miles. Three sides overlooked the water. The fourth side looked out over a forest aflame with brilliant color.

"Oh, look at this." Sidney couldn't seem to get enough of the magnificent scenery. "I don't know about those run-down hotels you've enjoyed on your world travels, but this place has the most amazing view."

"Isn't it great?" He walked up beside her and watched as, far below, the wind whipped the waves into a frenzied dance, crashing onto the shore and sending foaming spray hundreds of feet into the air.

Far out on the horizon, puffs of smoke signaled an ore carrier struggling against wind and waves on its way to port.

Sidney was entranced by the slap of light rain against the panes, and the whitecaps churning the lake into an angry brew. "How I'd love to capture that on canvas."

Adam arched an eyebrow. "If you'd like, I'll get your gear and set it up right here."

"Don't be silly. I wouldn't impose on you like that."

"It's not an imposition. It'll only take minutes. Besides, I understand the need to capture something that affects you so strongly. I've had the urge a few times myself." And was fighting an urge of his own, just being this close to her. He welcomed the chance to give them both a distraction.

She glanced at the darkening sky. "I'll need to head home soon or it'll be too dark to find my way."

"I'll drive you when you're ready to go."

She was chewing on her lip, torn between being sensible and giving in to the need to paint this scene. "You wouldn't mind?"

He was already heading out the door, calling over his shoulder, "Don't move. I'll be right back."

Sidney worked quickly, afraid that the last of the light would soon be gone and this magnificent view lost forever. Even if she should return on another day, the lake would never look the way it did now, all rough, tumbling waves beneath an angry, brooding sky.

She mixed paint on her palette before layering it on the canvas in strong, bold strokes.

Though the room was cold, she took no notice as she added yet another color to the waves, giving them just a hint of the darkness that lay beneath.

Picasso and Toulouse had long ago tired of investigating their new surroundings and had settled down at her feet. The dog snored softly while the cat carefully groomed himself.

Sidney had no idea how much time had passed since she'd first started. She knew only that she didn't want this to end. Having a room made of glass, with the sea, the sky and the forest around her, was an artist's idea of heaven.

She added more paint, then sat back to view her work. Though she would need to add more darkness to those leaden clouds, and a few more touches of white and silver to the foam that capped the waves, she had caught the essence of the power and majesty of this great lake. It could look deceptively gentle in summer, with water as smooth as glass, shimmering beneath a canopy of puffy clouds. But in autumn, when the north wind began its chill dance, Lake Michigan showed another facet of its ever-changing personality. Here was the monster that had become a legend in these parts. In days of old it had tossed ships about like toys, forcing crews to abandon their treasure in the caves that dotted the shore. Even now, with all their modern technology, ships and sailors found themselves at the mercy of Great Lakes storms. Seasoned sailors swapped stories about the vicious storms that could blow up in the Great Lakes without warning, surpassing anything they might encounter anywhere else in the world.

Adam poked his head in the door, causing the dog to roll over and open its eyes and the cat to pause in the act of licking one paw. "How's it going?"

Sidney's smile was radiant. "Want to take a look?"

He crossed the room to stand directly behind her. When the silence stretched out too long, Sidney turned to glance at him.

He was staring intently at the canvas. "It's wonderful."

The pleasure in his voice warmed her as nothing else could have.

"Thank you. And thank you for allowing me to intrude on your space, Adam."

"You didn't intrude." He watched as she stood, pressing a hand to the small of her back. "But I think I should have suggested that you take a break earlier. In fact, I thought about it and came up here, only to find you enjoying yourself so much, I was reluctant to interrupt the flow."

"If you had tried, you'd have had a tiger on your hands."

"Yeah." He was grinning. "That's what I thought. Never disturb an artist in the act of creating a masterpiece. Since you have a habit of forgetting the time, I decided to feed you."

"Really?" She turned to him with a smile. "More chili?"

"Come on. I'll show you." He led her toward the door, with the dog and cat trailing in their wake.

Downstairs, the logs blazing on the hearth made the room warm and inviting. The wooden bench that served as a coffee table had been set with two plates and a variety of covered dishes. To one side stood a bottle of pale wine and two stem glasses.

Adam filled the glasses and handed one to her.

"Thank you." She sipped and realized, as she

glanced at the window, that darkness had fallen and the rain had picked up to a steady, pounding drone. "How many hours was I up there?"

Adam shrugged. "I didn't bother to keep track. All I know is that I looked in on you a couple of times and you never even heard me, you were so deep into that zone."

He held up two bowls of pet food. "I'm taking a page from your book." The minute he set the dishes by the fire, they were quickly attacked by the hungry dog and cat.

"You seem to have thought of everything." She glanced at the covered dishes. "How could you have possibly found the time to do all this?"

"Easy." He led her over to the sofa and waited until she'd taken a seat before lifting the lid on the first dish to reveal perfectly breaded and browned lake perch and steaming baked potatoes. "I drove into town and picked it all up at The Pier."

"Oh, Adam." She was shaking her head as he sat beside her and began serving their plates. "I can't imagine a more wonderful surprise."

"I'm happy to oblige, ma'am." He tasted his wine and watched as she dug into her meal before joining her. After one bite he sighed. "The owner, Claire Huntington, assured me I couldn't go wrong with the perch. And she was right."

"It's one of my favorites."

"So she told me."

Sidney's head came up sharply. "You told her you were buying this for me?"

"For us." He paused a beat. "Does that bother you?"

"Of course not." But her protest sounded feeble even to her own ears. "It's just that Devil's Cove is such a small town. I'd hate to have Claire thinking we're…" Her voice trailed off.

"We're enjoying one another's company? Would that be so wrong?"

"Certainly not. We're two adults."

"But…"

She sighed. "There's a lot of curiosity about me, living alone out in the woods. I suppose the fact that I'm an artist adds to the speculation. And now my nearest neighbor is the town's handsome mystery man living in the lighthouse."

His grin was quick and dangerous. "You think I'm handsome?"

She couldn't help laughing aloud. "Hard to tell under all that facial hair."

At the quirk of his eyebrow she gave another laugh. "As if you don't know you're handsome. I'm sure you've used those looks to cast a spell on dozens of women."

"Hundreds. But who's counting?" He topped off her wine and sat back. "Do you really care what the people in town say or think about you?"

"I shouldn't, I know. And for the most part I

don't really give it much thought. But a part of me is still that girl who grew up here.''

He nodded in understanding. ''And you don't want to be the object of town gossip.''

''Exactly.''

''But since you are, why not just resign yourself to the inevitable?''

''Is that what you'd do?''

He sipped his wine. ''It would seem to me, once resignation sets in, the rest is easy. Now why don't we both relax and enjoy the evening.''

''Oh, Adam, how could I not?'' She buttered a roll while eyeing the two slices of cheesecake. ''Especially when I see what you brought for dessert.''

He gave her a mocking leer. ''Hmm. Now that I know your weakness, my pretty, I can easily have my way with you. After all, how can you resist a handsome mystery man who offers you cheesecake?''

They shared a laugh as they finished their dinner.

Adam set aside his napkin. ''Would you care for more wine, or would you prefer coffee with dessert?''

''Coffee, please, especially since I can smell it brewing in the kitchen, and it's making me weak.'' She watched him walk away and sat back, sipping the last of her wine as she realized that it wasn't the smell of coffee that was affecting her, but this man. This place. This night.

He seemed different tonight. Some of the tension she'd sensed in him from their first meeting seemed to have dissipated. He'd actually been able to relax enough with her to share a few laughs.

He returned with a tray holding two mugs and a carafe, as well as cream and sugar. After setting it down he handed her a steaming mug.

"Now for dessert. But first..." He spooned fresh strawberries over the cheesecake and drizzled it with warm strawberry preserves.

At Sidney's arched eyebrow he explained. "I had strict orders from the owner to serve this exactly as they do at The Pier, for the best possible effect."

"Effect?" She set down her mug to stare at him.

"Yeah. I am, after all, trying to appease you."

"Appease?"

"For knocking you off your bike and giving you that shiner." He met her look. "Is it working?"

"Oh, yes." She couldn't help laughing. "So far, I'm very appeased. And impressed. But maybe I'd better taste that cheesecake before I give a final verdict." She took a tiny bite, just to tempt herself, and couldn't hold back the little sigh that escaped her lips as she took a second, bigger taste. "Oh, this is sinful."

"Why are all the really pleasurable things in life given that label?" He helped himself to a generous bite, then another, before turning to her.

She sat back, listening to the rain pelting the windows, and the hiss and snap of the fire on the hearth. At the moment she felt warm and snug and content. "That's a good question. But after this much pleasure...I mean sinful pleasure...I'm out of answers."

He took her hand in his, staring for long seconds at the long, tapered artist's fingers, before looking up into her eyes with a smile. "I know what you mean." Linking his fingers with hers he leaned back and stretched out his long legs toward the warmth of the fire. "I can't remember when I've spent a more peaceful day."

"Does that count as sinful, too?"

He saw the smile that curved her lips and thought about how desperately he wanted to taste them again.

He nodded toward the two animals, dozing in front of the fire. "I think Picasso and Toulouse like it here."

"What's not to like?" She could feel the heat of his touch burning a path of fire along her arm.

Outside, the wind and rain picked up, beating on the windows. It seemed the most natural thing in the world for Adam to turn toward her and lean close until their lips were mere inches apart.

She waited, afraid to breathe, until his mouth brushed hers. Except for a quick hitch of breath, she sat perfectly still, absorbing the rush of feelings that shuddered through her as his arms came around her and he drew her firmly against him. All the while he continued plundering her mouth with his, drinking her in like a man starved for the taste of her.

She thought this time she would be prepared for the heat, and she was. But nothing could prepare her for the rush of needs. Needs so fierce, she actually trembled.

Despite the alarm bells that were sounding a warning, Adam took the kiss deeper, unwilling to end this just yet.

''You taste like strawberries,'' he whispered as he drew her even closer. ''And I've never been able to resist strawberries.''

She put a hand to his chest and drew back, taking in deep drafts of air. ''I need a minute.''

He caught her hand between both of his and stared into her eyes, as though trying to read her thoughts. ''I need a whole lot more than a minute.'' He seemed to consider his words carefully. ''I know I promised to drive you home. And I will, if that's what you want. But since we're so cozy in here, you might want to consider the miserable weather we'll be forced to endure out there.''

''Are you asking me to spend the night?''

He released her hand before giving a quick slap to his forehead. ''The devil made me do it. Forget I even mentioned it.''

She was amazed that she was able to laugh, when only seconds before she'd felt brittle, fragile enough to break into little pieces. But now her laughter rang out, clear as a bell. "I believe they wrote a song about that."

It took him a moment to understand. "Guilty. But it's true, you know. Baby, it's not only cold outside, it's pouring rain."

"I won't melt."

"Maybe not. But I will if you kiss me like that one more time. Would you like to see it?"

"I'm not sure it would be a pretty sight to see a man melt." She sighed and got to her feet. "I really do think it's time to get home."

"I can't change your mind?"

She managed a smile. "I'm sure you could. That's why I'd like to leave now."

The minute she stood up, Picasso and Toulouse left their spots by the fire and began circling her feet.

"Eager to get home, boys?" she called.

In response they ran to the door.

"Traitors." Adam picked up a jacket and went in search of his car keys. "I thought all men were supposed to stick together."

Chapter 6

Sidney sat in front of the fire sipping hot chocolate, watching the morning sunlight making shifting patterns on the hearth. But it wasn't the pretty scene that had her attention, it was thoughts of Adam. Though she hadn't seen him in a week, since that night at the lighthouse, he'd been on her mind, and had caused her to lose a great deal of sleep. She'd wanted more than anything to spend the night with him. It had been on the tip of her tongue to agree to his offer, but something had held her back.

Guilt, she realized. She felt guilty for wanting to live again, while Curt lay cold in his grave. A completely irrational thought, she knew, but there it was. She was a smart woman. She knew that she'd been avoiding any serious relationship since Curt's death, because it was easier to live alone. If she allowed herself to feel again, to possibly love again, she would also be opening herself up to be hurt again.

Everyone had told her that the pain of loss would subside, and that in time she would be able to move on with her life. Though her heart was aching, she'd heeded their advice and had given herself the time needed to heal. She had moved on, but she'd never forgotten. And though the sharp edge of pain was gone, there remained a dull ache, a shadow to remind her of her loss. She'd vowed to never open herself up to that kind of suffering again.

And here she was, debating the wisdom of sleeping with a man who was practically a stranger. What did she know about Adam Morgan except that he was a man without roots. Hadn't he boasted of it? A man without a place to call home. A world traveler who never knew where his next assignment would take him. A rolling stone happily poised to follow a new trail as soon as the opportunity arose.

She was a woman who needed, more than anything, a sense of permanence in her life. This cottage, this town, held her heart. She'd known after a year in Tuscany, one of the most beautiful places in the world, that she needed to return to her roots more than she needed the inspiration of a lovely setting or the pursuit of another's dream.

After the initial shock of Curt's death had begun

to recede, she'd been able to find peace and joy in her life again, by concentrating solely on her work. If she'd had to repress her sexual appetite, it hadn't mattered, for she'd found even more passion than ever in her art.

Now, that sexual hunger was back. If possible, it was stronger than ever. If Adam's passionate kisses at the lighthouse weren't enough, his long, possessive kiss good-night at her door that night had left her stunned and shaken, causing her to wonder again if she'd made the wrong choice by pushing him away. It had been on the tip of her tongue to ask him in to spend the night here.

Instead, she'd said nothing. Merely watched him drive away, and had then retired to her bed. Alone.

Alone.

The word played like a litany in her mind.

Her choice, she thought miserably. And because of that choice, she hadn't seen Adam in a week. Didn't that prove that he was as reluctant for a relationship as she was? And though she liked the fact that he was willing to accept her decision without argument, a little voice inside her head kept reminding her that a more persistent lover would have dogged her trail and would have done everything in his power to change her mind.

Was that what she really wanted? To be swept off her feet? To be so caught up in the thrill of passion that she couldn't think? To be carried mindlessly into an affair with no thought to the future?

That had been enough for her once. A college student with stars in her eyes and a courageous man who needed her desperately. A man who had clung to her like a lifeline. She could have no more refused Curt's insistence on marriage than she could have refused to breathe. But she'd undergone a complete transformation in the years since then. That sweet, innocent girl no longer existed. It had been a long, uphill battle, but she was in charge of her own life now, and she liked it that way. She had no intention of going back.

At a knock on the door Picasso and Toulouse raced across the room, waiting impatiently while she peered out. Seeing Adam, she pulled open the door as a thrill shot through her. At once the dog and cat danced circles at his feet, stirring up the red-and-gold leaves that covered the ground.

"Good morning." She wondered at the lightness around her heart at the mere sight of him. He needed a shave. His eyes looked tired and bloodshot. His hair was tousled from the wind. And there was no denying that he looked better to her than any knight in shining armor. "Come in."

Instead of stepping past her he paused on the threshold, his eyes steady on hers. "How've you been?"

"Fine." She marveled that her voice sounded so

normal, when her heart was doing somersaults inside her chest. "And you?"

"Miserable."

She couldn't control the smile of delight that curved her lips and sparkled in her eyes. "Poor baby. Why are you miserable?"

"I've been missing you."

"Well, then." She took a moment to quell the little dance her heart was doing. "It's a good thing one of us is fine."

He cupped her face in his hands. His voice was a low growl of anger. "I hope you're lying."

He leaned closer, and Sidney wondered that her poor heart didn't burst clear through her chest as she waited for his lips to claim hers.

Against her mouth the growl deepened to a snarl. "I can't stand to think I'm alone in this misery."

Before they could consummate their kiss they heard the sudden crunch of tires, and looked up to see a car moving slowly along the trail that led to her cabin. As soon as it came to a halt, Picasso and Toulouse were dancing around it, wriggling with excitement.

The doors opened and Sidney's mother and grandmother stepped out. Both women were staring with interest at the young woman and the rugged stranger standing so close their bodies were touching.

At their approach both Sidney and Adam stepped apart, wearing matching looks of guilt and dismay.

"Good morning, darling." Her mother hurried forward to brush a kiss over Sidney's cheek.

"Mom. Bert." Sidney embraced her grandmother. "Have you two met Adam Morgan?"

"We've never met, but as a member of the historical society, we've exchanged enough faxes to fill a ledger." Bert offered her handshake. "Hello, Adam. I'm Sidney's grandmother, Alberta Brennan, but everyone calls me Bert. And this is Sidney's mother, Charley."

He grinned as he shook hands. "Bert and Charley. Sounds like a comedy act I once saw in Chicago."

Charley's laughter rang on the breeze. "Now there's something we might want to consider in the future, Bert."

The two women were still laughing as Sidney held the door. "Why don't we all go inside and I'll make some hot chocolate."

She waited for the others to precede her. When Adam stepped past her he paused a moment to touch a hand to her shoulder. Just a touch, but she could feel the path of fire all the way to her heart.

Once inside Bert sniffed the air. "Something smells wonderful. Is that cinnamon?"

Sidney nodded. "It is. I made myself cinnamon toast for breakfast. I'll fix you some if you'd like."

"I'd love some." Bert turned to her daughter-in-law. "How about you, Charley?"

"Just the chocolate for me, thanks." Charley walked to the fireplace and stood a moment, absorbing the warmth of the fire. "Oh, Sidney, I love this cabin more every time I visit."

Sidney looked up from the stove with a smile. "So do I. I can't imagine feeling this comfortable anywhere else."

"It certainly suits you." Bert was busy scratching behind Picasso's ears, while Toulouse vied for her attention.

Minutes later Sidney carried a tray of steaming hot chocolate and buttered cinnamon toast to the coffee table. While the two women helped themselves, she carried a cup to Adam and absorbed his warmth as their fingers brushed. For the space of a heartbeat they exchanged intimate smiles, before Sidney crossed the room and sat in a rocker, draping an afghan over her legs. At once Toulouse settled himself on her lap and began purring, while Picasso took up his position in front of the fire beside Adam.

"What brings you out here so early in the morning?" Sidney's smile grew. "And don't try telling me you just happened to be passing by."

Charley chuckled. "We just wanted to see how you were getting along. And you're right. Our early arrival was planned. I told Bert if we didn't get here soon enough, you'd be off somewhere in the woods painting, and we'd never find you.''

Bert turned to Adam, who was kneeling on the hearth, scratching behind Picasso's ears. ''How is our lighthouse working out for you, Adam?''

''It's everything I'd hoped for. Despite its age, it's snug and comfortable.'' His gaze strayed to Sidney, idly petting her cat. ''How could anyone complain about the view around here? It's spectacular.''

Bert exchanged a quick look with Charley before setting her cup in its saucer. ''You saved us a trip to the lighthouse, Adam. You're the real reason we're here. We thought we'd have a visit with Sidney first, and then we'd planned on stopping by the lighthouse on our way back to town to see if you'd come to brunch at the Willows tomorrow.''

''Brunch?''

''It's a weekly affair at our place. Just our family, and a few honored guests. We've love to have you join us.''

''Thank you.'' He seemed to be considering before he nodded. ''I'd be happy to come.''

''Good. Be there around noon.'' Bert glanced at her granddaughter. ''Maybe you two could drive together. That would save you having to navigate those bumpy roads, Sidney.''

Sidney seemed puzzled by her grandmother's implication. ''I've navigated those roads for years without any problem. Why would you worry about me now?"

Seeing her prickly reaction, Adam couldn't hide the grin that split his lips. "I'd be happy to pick up Sidney. That way she can make certain that I don't get lost."

"There you are." Pleased with herself, Bert merely smiled. "I bet a man like you, who has traveled all over the world, doesn't get lost often."

"I see my reputation precedes me."

The older woman gave him what she hoped was a bland look. "As a member of the historical society, I was privy to certain information about our new tenant." She paused a beat. "Is it true that you've been in both Afghanistan and Iraq?"

He nodded, and though his smile remained, something flickered in his eyes.

Seeing it, Bert was quick to add, "I admire the men and women who put themselves in harm's way in order to let the rest of us know what goes on around the world."

"On behalf of those men and women, I appreciate the thought." His smile warmed. "But most of us do it because we love it, not because we see ourselves as some sort of hero."

"Another reason to admire your work, Adam. Too many of us do what is comfortable, rather than pursue what we truly desire. Even though, as a retired teacher I might have much to give to the children of other cultures, I'm afraid I'm far too complacent and comfortable to ever give up my life here to live and teach in a foreign land.''

Adam's voice lowered. ''Don't be too hard on yourself. From the little I've seen of Devil's Cove, I think I'd find it hard to leave, too.''

''Really?'' Bert exchanged another look with her daughter-in-law before getting to her feet. ''I think we'd better start back home now, Charley, and let these young people get to their work.''

''Of course.'' Sidney's mother drained her cup and set it on the tray. ''The hot chocolate was perfect, darling.'' She draped an arm around her daughter's shoulders as Sidney stood and walked with her to the door. ''I'm glad to see you looking so well. Don't you agree, Bert?''

The older woman gave a quick nod of her head. ''I do indeed. And I find it comforting to know you have a neighbor nearby in case of an emergency.''

''In a forest this large Adam can hardly be called a next-door neighbor, Bert.''

''Close enough.'' She paused on the threshold and smiled at Adam, still standing by the fireplace. ''I can't wait for you to meet the rest of Sidney's family tomorrow. Maybe you wouldn't mind sharing a few of your adventures.''

''I look forward to it.'' Adam watched as Sidney walked her mother and grandmother to their car.

When she returned, she stood in the window and

waved until they were out of sight. When she turned, Adam was grinning.

"What's that smile for?"

"Your family. They're fascinating. And transparent as glass. They were sizing me up."

She didn't bother to deny it. "I think they were more than a little intrigued when they drove up and found us here together at such an early hour. For all they know, we might have spent the night together."

"Is that what they're thinking?"

"It's hard to know what they're thinking. They certainly didn't say a word about it to me when we walked outside just now. But you have to admit we looked awfully intimate standing there by the front door, practically crawling into each other's skin."

"What a pleasant thought." He crossed to her, his voice lowering with implied intimacy. "And I say, if we're going to be damned for something we didn't do, why not at least have the satisfaction of doing it?" He nodded toward her bedroom. "There's still time to take me up on the offer I made last time we were together."

She pretended to glance at her watch. "Sorry. The morning's almost gone. I have work to do."

He gave her a wolfish grin. "Okay. Go paint some wildly exotic canvas that will bring you ridiculous piles of money." He brushed a kiss over her cheek. "But at least tell me you had to think about my offer for more than a minute before turning me down.''

She had to swallow hard before she could speak. She forced a light tone. ''Oh, believe me. I had to agonize all of two or three minutes before I could refuse such a wonderful, generous offer as yours.''

He started toward the door, then paused. ''There's always tonight. How about dinner?''

''You know where that would lead.''

''That's what I'm hoping.''

She hadn't a doubt. Which was why she was relieved that she'd already made plans. ''Sorry. I can't tonight, Adam. I've already made plans with my sister Courtney to meet with a group of art patrons.''

''Do you do that often?''

She shook her head. ''This is special. They've offered to make a very generous donation to the Devil's Cove Artists Society in exchange for a chance to meet and talk with their favorite local artist.''

''I don't blame them. Maybe my best chance at spending time with my favorite local artist is to make that same offer.''

She laughed. ''You can try. Or you can join the local art patrons tonight at Courtney's shop.''

He shook his head. ''As lovely as it sounds, I'd rather not have to watch you from afar while the adoring crowds worship at your feet.''

''That sounds delightful. I'll let you know if it

ever happens.'' She laughed. ''But I will take you up on your offer to drive me to the Willows tomorrow.''

''Deal.'' He opened the door, then surprised her by closing it and returning to her side. ''If I can't have tonight, at least let me have this.''

Without waiting for her reply he dragged her into his arms and kissed her long and slow and deep. When at last he lifted his head, he gave her a smoldering look before turning away and crossing the room. This time when he pulled open the door he stepped outside and resolutely closed it behind him.

Sidney stood perfectly still, waiting for her heart to settle back to its natural rhythm.

Had she imagined it, or had the floor actually tilted when Adam kissed her?

She dropped to her knees and picked up Toulouse, rubbing her chin over the cat's fur. ''I think I'm in way over my head, Toulouse. What am I going to do about Adam Morgan?''

In answer the cat merely yawned and closed its eyes, purring contentedly.

''You're no help at all.'' Sidney settled him on the afghan before picking up the tray of empty cups and carrying them to the kitchen.

An hour later she and her pets made their way through the forest to the water's edge, where Sidney set up her easel and stool and immersed herself in work.

Becoming absorbed in her work had always been enough to take her mind off her problems. But now, no matter how hard she tried to concentrate, she found thoughts of Adam flitting through her mind, causing her to pause, brush in hand, as a smile touched her lips.

She couldn't deny that, despite all her doubts and fears, she couldn't wait to see him again.

She shivered. She hadn't felt this delicious sense of excitement in years. This wonderful feeling of anticipation, as though something new and wondrous and life altering was waiting for her just around the corner.

Chapter 7

Sunday morning dawned misty and mild, without a trace of the rain that had been predicted.

As was her custom, Sidney took Picasso and Toulouse on a long hike through the woods, laughing at their antics as they scared up rabbits and squirrels, and even a fat groundhog that looked especially annoyed by the intrusion. By the time she returned to her cabin, the sun had broken through the curtain of mist, bathing everything in bright light.

Hearing the crunch of wheels along the trail, Sidney had the door open even before Adam's Jeep came to a halt.

Picasso and Toulouse raced outside to dance excitedly around his ankles, before accompanying him to the cabin.

Though Sidney resented the tingle of anticipation that flowed through her at the mere sight of Adam, she couldn't deny it. She was as happy as her dog and cat, and just as starved for his attentions.

She stared in surprise at the sight of him in charcoal cords and sweater, topped by a lighter gray sport coat. "How handsome you look." She touched a hand to his cheek. "You even shaved."

"Every now and then I do that. But only for very special occasions." He gave her a slow appraisal that had the heat rushing to her cheeks. "Now I'm glad I did. You look amazing."

With an ankle-skimming skirt and matching sweater set in pale buttercup cashmere, and her red hair plaited into one fat braid that spilled over her shoulder, she was more colorful than the autumn foliage that shimmered around her.

"Ready to go?"

She paused. "In a minute." She called Picasso and Toulouse inside before pulling the door shut.

As she followed Adam to his car she glanced toward the window, where the dog and cat stood watching with the most forlorn expressions.

Following the direction of her gaze Adam burst into laughter. "I've never known a pair of animals that could express so much emotion. Look at their sad faces."

She joined in the laughter. "They do this every

time I leave them. Poppie calls it playing on my sympathy. They really know how to get to me.''

''That's because they have you pegged as a softie.'' He helped her inside before settling himself in the driver's seat. He turned the key in the ignition, but instead of putting the vehicle in gear, he lifted her hand to his lips. ''And they're not the only ones. You've got a tender heart, Sidney. I find that very endearing.''

When he released her hand and turned his attention to maneuvering the Jeep along the rutted path, Sidney sat back and wondered at the feelings assaulting her. How was it that his mere touch could turn her knees to jelly?

He kept his eyes on the path. ''Tell me about this brunch.''

Sidney smiled. ''I'm not sure it's something I can describe. I guess it's just something you have to experience to believe.''

''Who will be there?''

''My family.''

''All of them?''

She nodded. ''They wouldn't miss it. Unless there's a dire emergency, everyone will be there. My sisters and their husbands. My mother, of course, and my grandparents. You'll get to witness the ongoing battle of wills between Poppie and the housekeeper, Trudy, who claims to detest every one of his inventions.''

"He's an inventor? I thought he was a retired judge."

"He's both. But he's very proud of his inventions, which he insists will, if not revolutionize the world, at least make Trudy's job easier. The only problem with that is Trudy intentionally misplaces them as quickly as possible so she won't have to put up with them."

"I think I'm going to enjoy watching the show."

"Oh, I guarantee it."

She looked up in surprise when the lighthouse loomed ahead of them. "This isn't the way to the highway."

"I know. I've decided to pick up my gear. I think I'd like some shots of you in that outfit. Who knows? You may find yourself in the historical society's annual almanac."

He was out of the Jeep in seconds, leaving the engine running. Minutes later he bounded from the lighthouse with a bulging duffel slung over his shoulder.

"What could you possibly need with all that?" She watched him stow it in the back of the vehicle.

"I can't tell you how many times I've been ready to shoot a scene and discovered that the particular lens I wanted has been left behind." He climbed in and put the Jeep in reverse. "So over the years I've learned that it's just easier to bring everything in one big bag than do without the one thing I need."

She was shaking her head. "All that equipment for a few simple pictures."

"Maybe they won't be simple. Maybe I'll decide to ask you to pose for hours until I get the perfect shot."

She laughed. "And maybe I'll just refuse, and you'll have gone to all this trouble for nothing."

He shot her a sideways glance. "I'd love to have you pose nude for me in the light tower."

"In your dreams."

He was smiling, but there was a subtle change in his tone. "You'd blush if you could see inside my dreams, Sidney."

"I'm not sure I'd want to." Though she kept her voice light, she couldn't help shivering.

"I already have some pictures of you, of course. I had them developed in town, and I'm thinking of framing them."

"When did you take them?"

"When you were painting by the shore."

She wondered at the feelings that rippled through her. There was something intriguing about the thought of Adam snapping shots of her while she was completely unaware.

"How did I look?"

He chuckled. "Are you fishing for compliments?"

She shrugged. "Maybe. Was I cold? Wind-blown?"

"You were absolutely gorgeous. I couldn't take my eyes off you. The camera loves you, by the way. There isn't a bad shot in the entire roll. I'll show them to you one day."

As they turned off the dirt road onto the highway that led to town, Sidney drew in a long, satisfied breath. "I never tire of seeing Devil's Cove."

"It's a pretty town."

"Yes, it is. But it's more than just a pretty town. It's filled with good people. Most of whom, by the way, I've known all my life."

He gave a shake of his head. "I know you can't understand, but I find myself constantly amazed at the fact that you live in a town where you grew up, knowing all the people your whole life."

"No more amazing than the fact that you call everywhere home, and can be perfectly comfortable among strangers."

They fell silent as they drove along the main street, past the shops and restaurants which in summer teemed with tourists. Now there was no more than a trickle of visitors, who came to enjoy the autumn scenery.

Sidney pointed up ahead to the row of lovely old houses that stood along the shore. "We'll follow this street to the Willows." Moments later she pointed again. "Here's our place."

Adam turned the car up a long curving driveway and came to a halt behind several other cars.

"It looks like everyone is here ahead of us." Sidney accepted Adam's hand as she stepped from the car.

Together they followed the sound of voices to the other side of the house.

"Does this mean we're eating outside?"

Sidney nodded. "The patio. It's Poppie's favorite spot. And since there are so few days like this left, I'm sure he's eager to take advantage of it."

"What does he do in winter?"

"He rules like an emperor in the formal dining room," she said in a whisper. "And drives Trudy crazy."

As they walked, Adam studied the ivy-covered brick-and-stone facade, the slate-tiled roof that rose above three stories and the graceful curve of walkways still lush with hardy autumn flowers and colorful shrubs.

When they came around the side of the house, he could see the sweep of lawn that ran all the way to the water's edge and the lovely brick-paved patio. The furniture was a mix of wicker and glass, with brightly colored cushions on the chairs and gliders. Adding even more color were urns filled with waving grasses and pots of mums.

Adam leaned close to whisper, "You forgot to tell me you grew up in a mansion."

"Did I?" She merely smiled as she drew him forward.

"About time." The voice was as scratchy as a rusty gate.

Adam paused to study the woman speaking. She was as wide as she was tall, with tufts of white-cotton curls around a face with eyes like a blackbird.

She caught Sidney's arm and leaned close. "The Judge is trying out his newest contraption. If you ask me, it's just like all the others. A silly waste of his time and mine."

"I'm sure you'll find a use for it. Trudy, I'd like you to meet our guest, Adam Morgan."

Those dark eyes shifted to the man beside Sidney, looking him over as carefully as she might examine a tray of prime ribs to be served to royalty.

Suddenly her eyes crinkled and her lips curved into an almost wicked grin. "Well, this day has certainly started to improve. You the photographer living in the lighthouse?"

"That's me." Adam offered his hand and she wiped hers on her apron before accepting.

"And you're here with our Sidney." She stared into his eyes, her smile growing. "Nice to meet you, Adam. I have a feeling I'll be seeing you around."

She turned away and walked back to the house.

Adam leaned close to mutter, "No shrinking violet there. For a minute I had the feeling she saw me as brunch and was wondering just how to cook me."

"Goose, no doubt," Sidney said with a laugh. "Trudy is very good at cooking everyone's goose."

They were still chuckling when Frank Brennan looked up from the grill and spotted them.

"Here you are." He set aside giant tongs and hurried over to take Sidney's hands in his. "Now we're all together."

"Poppie." Sidney wrapped her arms around his neck and hugged him fiercely before turning to include Adam. "I'd like you to meet Adam Morgan."

"A pleasure, Adam. Welcome to our home."

"Thank you, sir. From what I've seen of it, it's beautiful."

"I'll see that Sidney gives you a tour before you leave. I understand you've already met Bert and Charley." The old man drew his wife close and kept one arm around her shoulders. "Now I'd like you to meet the rest of our family." He turned to include the others who had gathered close. "This is my granddaughter Emily, who has now taken our son Christopher's position as town doctor, and her husband, Jason Cooper."

Adam returned their handshakes. "I've been looking forward to meeting the town doctor, Emily. And nobody needs to tell me about Jason Cooper." He turned to the man beside her. "I've read all your books. They kept me sane when the world around me went crazy."

"That's nice to know." Jason smiled. "I happen

to be a fan of yours, as well. I've long admired your photos. Especially that one of the Afghan children that won you the Pulitzer.''

Sidney watched Adam's reaction to her brother-in-law's words. He seemed actually embarrassed that someone had recognized him.

''Did you think no one here in Devil's Cove would know your name?'' she asked.

Adam gave a half-hearted shrug. ''I guess I was hoping to be anonymous.''

''That would be hard to do with a reputation like yours. You had to assume that sooner or later someone would connect your name to that award.''

Adam merely grinned. ''It rarely comes up in conversations. I've never learned how to say, 'Hi, I'm Adam Morgan, Pulitzer prize-winning photographer.'''

That had everyone laughing.

The Judge continued his introductions. ''Adam, this is our granddaughter Hannah and her husband Ethan, and those two little imps running through the piles of leaves are their two sons, Danny and T.J.''

''I've seen your landscaping signs all over town, Hannah.'' Adam exchanged handshakes with the adults and winked at the two boys who waved their chubby hands as they ran past, chasing falling leaves.

Frank Brennan turned. ''And yet another granddaughter, Courtney and her husband Blair Colby.''

"That pretty little gift shop in town is yours, I believe?"

She dimpled. "And the lovely clubhouse being built at the country club is Blair's design."

"I've seen it. It's impressive." After more handshakes Adam shook his head. "This is quite an array of talent. Do all of you live here in town?"

"Most of the time." Jason brushed a kiss on Emily's cheek. "If I can get my wife to find another doctor to cover her practice for a while, I'd like to take her to Malibu to see if there's anything she'd like to bring back here before I put my house on the market." He glanced at Adam. "You wouldn't happen to be interested in buying a house in California, would you?"

"Sorry." Adam shook his head. "I have no desire to sink roots. But if I did, Malibu is the last place I'd choose to do it."

"I would have thought—" Frank glanced at his granddaughter Sidney, standing quietly beside Adam "—that after a life spent chronicling war all over the globe, you'd be eager to settle down someplace serene."

Adam arched an eyebrow. "I think about it from time to time, and then find myself going off on another assignment that leaves me little time to think about anything except staying out of harm's way. I guess serene just isn't part of my vocabulary."

Trudy wheeled a serving cart across the patio and

they gathered around, helping themselves to drinks. While the men gathered around the Judge, who was cooking on the grill, the women fell into the routine of helping Trudy set the table and carry various covered dishes from the kitchen to the patio.

As she worked beside the others Sidney glanced over to watch Adam laughing easily with her grandfather and brothers-in-law.

She felt an arm around her shoulders and glanced up to find her grandmother standing beside her.

"He's a fascinating man, isn't he?"

Sidney nodded.

"And secretive, it seems. Are you angry that he didn't tell you more about himself?"

"Not angry, Bert. But…embarrassed to find out so many things about him from what he told the others."

The older woman merely smiled. "Frankly, I find that sort of humility refreshing. There aren't many men who wouldn't find an opportunity to bring up their successes into every conversation."

"I suppose." Sidney sighed. "Still, I would have liked to know a little more about him. There seems to be so much he keeps to himself."

Bert brushed a strand of fiery hair from her granddaughter's cheek. "Would it have made any difference in the way you'd have treated him, my darling?"

Sidney shrugged. "I suppose not."

The old woman's voice lowered. Softened. ''Would it have made a difference in the way you feel about him?''

Sidney turned to study her grandmother with a look of mild disapproval. ''Why, Bert, I believe you're fishing.''

''And why not? I have every right to worry about you, Sidney.'' Bert cupped the young woman's face between her hands. ''How do you feel about Adam, darling?''

The sigh came from deep inside. ''I wish I knew. He's fascinating, daring, funny and charming, but he's also aloof and distant and keeps way too many secrets. Just when I think I'm starting to know him, I see another side to him that I don't even recognize.''

Hearing the depth of her distress, Bert leaned close to brush a kiss over Sidney's cheek. ''Time, darling. Give it time. We women aren't the only ones allowed to have our moods.''

Linking her arm through her granddaughter's, she drew her toward the table. ''Now if you don't mind, would you please arrange the flowers, Sidney. You know that none of us can do them as well as you.''

Sidney picked up the bouquet of pink and purple mums and began arranging them in an antique silver vase, using a few sprigs of vines and dried grasses for added texture and color. As she did, she continued to glance occasionally at Adam, trying to see him as her family did. But all she could see was that darkly handsome stranger who had stepped out of the woods and into her life, sipping a drink and exchanging pleasantries with her grandfather and the other men, listening, laughing and occasionally glancing her way. Whenever their gazes met, she felt a quick little thrill, as though, despite the distance between them, he'd actually touched her.

What did she know about Adam Morgan? No more than when she'd first met him. He was as secretive as ever, keeping his life and his accomplishments hidden from view.

Perhaps, she thought with a sigh, since he seemed so easy and natural with the others, she'd leave it to one of them to uncover a few of the secrets he seemed so determined to keep from her.

Men, she thought with a growing sense of frustration. One minute they made you the center of their universe. The next, you were not only out of sight, but out of mind, as well.

If only she could do the same with Adam. But even when he was out of sight, he seemed constantly on her mind.

Chapter 8

Sidney touched a napkin to her mouth. "I believe that may have been your best beef tenderloin ever, Poppie."

Her grandfather, seated at the head of the table, beamed. "Thank you, my dear. You may pass that thought along to Trudy, who wanted me to cook salmon again."

The housekeeper, busy circling the table to top off their cups of coffee, paused to give him a withering look. "Your own granddaughter is a respected doctor and she's the one who told me you should be eating more fish and less red meat."

"But not at my Sunday brunch, surely."

"Especially at Sunday brunch. And don't call me Shirley."

That had everyone around the table groaning at the old joke. These two had been playing out the same scene for over forty years and never seemed to tire of the mock battle.

Jason Cooper glanced across the table at Adam, seated next to Sidney. "I remember seeing a photo spread by you in one of the newsmagazines recently. You seemed to be in the thick of war."

Adam gave a negligent shrug of his shoulders. "All the news that's fit to print."

"What about the news your network deems unfit to print?"

Adam merely smiled. "I'm saving those shots for one of the many books I'm planning when I retire from being a war correspondent."

"And when would that be?" Blair chimed in.

Adam held a platter while Sidney helped herself to another slice of tenderloin. Seeing the way she glanced at him, his tone softened. "I guess when I decide I've had my fill of misery."

"It has to be a tough job." Emily sipped her coffee. "I've often thought about the medical personnel who travel to war-torn countries and try to help those who've been injured. It's something I've considered doing, at least for a few months."

"Every little bit makes a difference." Adam gave her a rare smile. "If everyone would give just a little of their time and talent, think what it would mean to people who've never known anything but violence.''

Ethan glanced at his two boys, enjoying Trudy's hot chocolate topped with creamy marshmallow. ''I'd be interested in hearing your take on the current troubles in the world, since it will certainly affect their futures.''

''I'd be the last one you'd want to hear from.'' Adam ducked his head. ''I'm not interested in anyone's politics. What I find myself caring deeply about are the innocent people who get caught in the cross fire. If you ask them, they don't care much for politics, either. They just want to live in peace and raise their children up to be good people.''

Intrigued, Hannah regarded Adam over the rim of her cup. ''You must have found yourself in some pretty dangerous situations. Have you ever been afraid?''

He saw the way Sidney turned to study him. ''Sure, I've been afraid. I'd have to be brain-dead not to know fear when I'm in the middle of a war zone. But I've never been paralyzed by it. I just do what I have to at the time, and worry about the right or wrong of it later.''

Courtney picked up her sister's thread. ''Does the danger keep you awake at night?''

''Not really. Trust me. After hiking miles over mountains until you're bone weary, or hitching a ride on a copter over some steamy jungle that has

your clothes stuck like glue, you could sleep standing up. Besides, since we usually can't drink the
water, we make up for it by drinking gallons of local
beer. That would put an insomniac to sleep instantly."

That had everyone laughing, including Trudy,
who had paused to listen in silence. Now she circled
the table holding up a serving tray. "Anyone ready
for seconds of my cinnamon-streusel coffee cake?"

"I wish I had room," Adam said. "I think that
was the best I've ever tasted, Trudy."

"Then I'll see that I have some wrapped for you
to take with you."

At the unexpected tone of her voice, Sidney
glanced over. Judging from the way the housekeeper
was beaming it was obvious that Adam's words of
praise had touched the old woman's heart. Besides,
Trudy had always had a soft spot in her heart for
men who walked on the wild side.

Sidney leaned over to whisper, "Aren't you the
sly one? Now she'll spend an entire winter baking
your favorite things."

He winked, sending her heart into a quick spiral.
"Maybe that's what I was counting on."

"Anyone else?" Trudy called. "Going once. Going twice…"

Even Danny and T.J., who rarely passed up a
chance for more sweets, had to shake their heads at

second helpings before dancing away to chase the colored leaves blowing across the lawn.

"All right then." Trudy began pushing the serving cart toward the French doors that led to the kitchen. "I'll leave you to your coffee."

As the others began to push away from the table, Bert stepped up beside Adam and looped her arm through his. "Let's walk off our food, shall we?"

Recognizing that she wanted a chance to speak with him in private, Adam placed a hand over hers, matching his steps to hers. They walked in silence across the lawn, following the slate stepping-stones that marked a trail from the patio to the very edge of the water. There they walked along the sandy shore and turned to see the Willows bathed in bright autumn sunlight.

Bert smiled. "I never tire of this sight."

"Sidney tells me you've been here for more than fifty years."

The old woman nodded. "That must seem such a long time to you. But Frank and I are constantly amazed at how quickly those years have flown by." She turned to look up at him. "You'll say the same thing one day."

"If I live long enough."

Though he said the words lightly, she sensed something more in his tone. "You were careful to give us only the highlights of your job, Adam, but

I have to assume that there's a great deal of danger in what you do.''

"No more so than the soldiers who have to fight, or the people who have to live through the terror of war right in their own neighborhoods.''

"Perhaps. But they have little choice. You, on the other hand, could refuse an assignment, couldn't you?''

He shrugged. "I could.''

"You seem to have little fear.''

Again that shrug. "There's danger everywhere. I could get killed crossing a busy street. I resigned myself years ago to live my life as I wanted, without giving in to the fear of what might happen.''

Bert's face creased into a smile. "I've always admired that attitude in a person, Adam.''

"Thank you, ma'am.''

She looked up at him with a smile. "You're not comfortable calling me Bert?''

He laughed. "Not yet. Maybe when I've known you longer.'' He paused a moment before adding, "But no matter how long I know your husband, I'll never call the Judge Poppie.''

That had them both laughing.

Even from this distance, Bert could make out Sidney's profile, as she stood talking with her mother and sisters. "What do you think of my granddaughter?''

"She's a beautiful woman.''

"Indeed she is."

"A gifted artist."

Bert nodded.

"I sense that she's comfortable with her own company. And she seems truly happy to be following her dream." He paused. "But I don't think that's what you really want to know, is it?"

When Bert merely smiled, he nodded. "All right. To answer the question you're reluctant to ask, I'll tell you this. I'm mad about her, and have been since I first saw her. But I'm trying very hard not to act on my feelings."

"Why?"

He chose his words carefully. "I'm not sure I can be what Sidney wants or needs."

"And what is that?"

"A man willing to sink roots here in Devil's Cove and live happily ever after the way her grandparents have."

"That wouldn't be enough for you, Adam?"

"I don't know the answer to that. Before I came here, I'd have said it was impossible. Now that my life has slowed down, and I've become dazzled by a certain red-haired angel, I'm beginning to think anything is possible. But I won't make her a promise I can't keep."

"An honest man." Bert paused and touched a hand to his cheek. "It isn't just your attitude I like,

Adam. It's you, as well. You're a good man. And a bright one. I think you'll figure it all out.''

"You may be giving me more credit than I deserve.''

She merely smiled.

They both looked up when Frank Brennan walked over to join them. "I believe you've monopolized our guest long enough. It's my turn.'' He pointed to the shed that was surrounded by a thick hedge of deep red sumac bushes, with their lush purple cones. "I'd like to show you my laboratory, Adam, where I work on my inventions.''

"I'd like to see it.'' Adam squeezed Bert's hands. "Will you let Sidney know where I've gone?''

"Of course.'' The old woman turned to her husband with a knowing look. "You're not to grill our houseguest, Frank.''

He shot her a look of complete innocence. "How could you even suggest such a thing, Bert?''

"Because I know you better than I know myself.'' She walked away shaking her head.

The two men walked in silence to the shed. Once inside, Frank switched on an overhead light, which filled the room with unexpectedly bright light, and strolled toward his workbench, littered with bits of wood and metal and an odd assortment of tools.

"I've always liked tinkering. It helps me sort through problems.'' He leaned his back against the workbench and studied Adam. "What do you like to do when you're not working?"

"It's always been photography for me. My work is my pleasure."

"You're a lucky man, to be doing what you love. I wonder, though, how you can take pleasure in filming war."

"It wasn't my first choice to chronicle war. I just happened to be in the wrong place at the wrong time when I did my first assignment. But now I like to think that by being there, by showing the world what's happening, I can keep both sides honest. Or at least as honest as anyone can be during wars and uprisings." Adam shrugged. "To escape from the horrors of war, I like to photograph the children. There's something so resilient about them."

The older man nodded. "I know what you mean. Whenever I found myself embroiled in a tough criminal trial, I could always find solace in my grandchildren. There's something about little girls that just tug at the heartstrings." He met Adam's eyes. "Some, I'm afraid, more than others."

The two men fell into an uncomfortable silence for a moment before Frank cleared his throat. "I may be retired from the bench, but I'm still an avid fan of criminal proceedings. I was fascinated by a particularly heinous assassination in New York City some months ago."

When Adam remained silent, the Judge folded his

arms over his chest. "As far as I can recall, the assassin has never been identified and is still at large."

Adam gave a curt nod of his head. "I'm afraid that's so."

"It was reported that several attempts have been made on the life of the only known witness to the crime."

"I can see that there's nothing wrong with your powers of observation, Judge Brennan."

Again that strained silence hung between them before the older man said, "If I was able to figure it out, so can the man who wants you dead."

Adam let out a long, slow breath. "Yeah. That idea has crossed my mind."

"Understand," the old man said softly, "that I like you, son, and wish you well. But my chief concern must be Sidney. Or haven't you given any thought to her safety?"

"Sidney is all I've thought about." Adam frowned. "You may find this hard to believe, but I've been working really hard at keeping my distance from her. Unfortunately, she has a mind of her own, and she can be very persuasive."

For the first time the older man chuckled. "It's the curse of the Brennans. The first time I met her grandmother, I knew she was the woman I would spend the rest of my life with. I just hadn't quite figured out how to persuade her to agree."

The two men shared a knowing smile.

Frank Brennan's smile faded. "Have you told Sidney about the threat that hangs over you?"

Adam shook his head. "I don't want her involved."

Frank sighed. "I'm afraid it's too late for that. Maybe you haven't seen the way she looks at you, but I have. I'd say she's become very involved. And that means, to my way of thinking, that you need to be forthright about the danger."

Adam clenched his hands at his sides. "I can try. There's no denying that until this man is apprehended, my life is in danger. I don't have a problem with that, because I realize it's the price I pay for the job I do. But I'm not particularly fond of putting those who have the misfortune of knowing me in the line of fire, as well."

"What about the authorities?"

"They're aware of where I am. And they're keeping an eye out. But as a man of the law, you have to know that the forces of evil have a way of sliding under, over, around or through whatever precautions the forces of good might use to try to keep us safe."

"That's very true. You sound like a man who has had to deal with such evil before."

"I've seen my share."

Frank lowered his voice. "I'm sure you have. And you've probably become adept at keeping yourself safe. But my concern here is Sidney. She's very special.''

''I can appreciate…''

The old man held up his hand to stop him. ''I don't say this just because she's my granddaughter. All of us who know and love Sidney worry about her. She's always been—'' his voice wavered for a moment ''—very sweet and fragile.''

Adam was aware of the raw emotion in the older man's voice. ''Sir, I'll do everything in my power to see that Sidney isn't touched by the danger that stalks me.''

''Not good enough, Adam.'' Frank uncrossed his arms and faced Adam with a determined look. ''Her grandmother and I couldn't bear it if anything happened to her. She's been hurt enough.''

''Enough?'' Adam's eyes narrowed. ''What does that mean?''

Frank shook his head. ''It isn't my place to tell you that any more than it would be my place to tell Sidney what I've learned about you. If Sidney wants you to know, she'll tell you herself. But I advise you in the strongest possible terms to be completely honest and forthright. You must tell her the truth about why you are here, and the danger you may have exposed her to.''

Adam nodded slowly. ''You're pretty persuasive. Are you sure you were never a defense attorney?''

Frank Brennan flashed one of his famous smiles. "In my day I was one of the best."

"I should have known."

There was a knock on the door of the shed seconds before it was yanked open. Sidney stood framed in the doorway, glancing first at Adam, then at her grandfather. "What are you two doing, locked away in here on such a pretty day?"

"Just guy talk." Adam stuck out his hand. "It was nice talking with you, Judge Brennan. I appreciate your words of wisdom. I hope we can do this again some time."

"I hope so, too, son." Frank turned to his granddaughter. "I promised Adam a tour of the house. Why don't you take him indoors now and show him around. He might especially enjoy seeing your paintings in the library."

"All right." Sidney was looking into Adam's eyes. "And after that I've been thinking it would be a shame to waste all this sunshine. There are so few days like this left before winter blows in. If you're still interested, I thought I'd take you up on your offer to pose for some photos."

"If I'm interested?" He didn't touch her, but the look in his eyes was so intense, the old man standing to one side was all but scorched by the heat.

Frank cleared his throat, and they both looked up in surprise, as though unaware that he was still there.

"You might want to say your goodbyes to your mother and grandmother before leaving."

"Hmm? Oh, yes. Of course." With a smile Sidney leaned close to brush a kiss over her grandfather's cheek.

When they left the shed and walked across the patio to exchange words with the rest of the family, Frank remained where he was, watching Sidney and Adam.

Seeing the looks that passed between them should have brought him relief. It had been such a long time since his beloved Sidney had found someone to put that glow in her eyes. But his heart was heavy at the thought of the unknown danger that stalked Adam, and by implication Sidney, as well.

Of all his granddaughters, Sidney had always seemed the most sweet and shy and helpless. He'd told Adam she was fragile, for that was exactly the way he'd always seen her. Delicate crystal, that could be irreparably damaged by the slightest blow.

Why did someone like Sidney have to be attracted to a man like Adam, who seemed to enjoy tempting fate and chose to live each day on the very edge of danger?

Frank Brennan knew one thing with certainty. He wouldn't be able to draw a contented breath until the unknown assassin was identified and put away where he could do no more harm.

As long as such a madman was free to ply his hideous trade, there was a sword hanging over his beloved granddaughter's head. A sword that could slice the very heart of this family to shreds.

Chapter 9

"This is Poppie's study." After conducting a tour of the rest of the house, Sidney opened the double doors and stood aside, allowing Adam to precede her.

He'd been so quiet since leaving her grandfather's shed, she found herself trying desperately to draw him out. He seemed to have gone somewhere in his mind. A place where she couldn't reach him.

"I've always loved this room best. That's why I saved it for last. I love everything about it. The worn leather couches. The walls of legal books. The desk that belonged to Poppie's grandfather."

Adam circled the room, noting the framed photos of four little girls that stood in a place of honor on the highly polished desk. Frank Brennan's words played through his mind.

There's something about little girls that just tug at the heartstrings. Some, more than others.

Lost in thought, he bent to study their faces. Then, realizing that Sidney was watching, he managed a smile. "Look at you. Is that a paint smudge on your cheek?"

"Of course." Sidney walked over to stand beside him. "Even then, when I was no more than seven or eight, I was always into paint. It's all I ever wanted to do. While Emily was picking up stray animals and nursing them back to health, and Hannah was working with Poppie in the garden, Courtney and I were rummaging in the attic for treasures that she could restore and I could paint. By the time I was twelve, I'd copied almost every painting that hung on the walls of this house and presented them to my family for every occasion." She pointed to a framed miniature that stood on the mantel. "That's one I did for Poppie's birthday the year I was ten."

Adam picked it up and gave a whistle of approval. "I thought I'd be looking at some primitive attempt, but this is charming."

She dimpled. "Thank you. But it was a copy, so it was easy. It was later, when I started painting original works, that I learned how hard it was to find my own signature style."

Adam stood back to admire a series of her wildlife paintings that graced the walls. "It's as distinguishable as a fingerprint. Now that I've seen enough of your paintings, I'd recognize your work anywhere."

"Really?" Her smile grew.

"Yeah." He turned to her with a smoldering look. "In case I haven't told you, you're pretty amazing. And so is your family. Fun and funny. Diverse. Talented. And all of you a pleasure to be around."

She could feel the heat rush to her cheeks at his unexpected compliment. "So are you. I had no idea just how far you'd traveled, or the things you'd seen. I only wish…" She paused, embarrassed by what she'd almost revealed.

"Wish what?"

When she shook her head he moved closer to touch a hand to her cheek. "You started this. Now give it up, Sidney."

"It seems so petty to admit. You'll think me foolish, but I was more than a little disappointed that you were willing to reveal so much more to my family than you've ever told me."

He felt a twinge, and recognized it as guilt. "I don't like talking about myself."

"I can see that. But I felt resentful that my family knew so much more about your work than I did. Jason had even seen a magazine spread of your photos, something I wasn't even aware of."

"Hey. Would you want me to go around boasting about all the things I'd accomplished?"

"Of course not. But it would be nice to know more about you than the fact that you work for WNN."

He framed her face with his hands and stared down into her eyes. The look he gave her had her blood heating. "Maybe it was deliberate on my part. I haven't wanted to talk about my work or the things I've seen. But now, seeing you with your family, having a chance to talk with your grandparents, I'm thinking that it's time I leveled with you about..."

They both looked up when a shadow fell over them, and saw Charley pausing in the doorway.

Seeing the way they stepped apart, she gave them both a gentle smile. "Sorry to intrude. I just came looking for you to say goodbye."

Sidney crossed to her mother and gave her a warm hug. "You could never intrude. Why are you leaving so soon on this lovely Sunday afternoon?"

"I have an appointment that I have to keep." Charley brushed a kiss over her daughter's cheek, then turned with a smile to Adam. "It was lovely seeing you again."

He took her hand between both of his. "I love your home here at the Willows, Charley. And your family."

"Thank you." She squeezed his hand, then turned away. "I'll call you later in the week, Sidney."

With a tap of heels on the polished hardwood floor, she was gone.

Hearing the sound of doors opening and closing, and voices drawing close, Adam lowered his voice. "I told your mother the truth. I do love your family. But I wouldn't mind finding some place less crowded where we could talk. There are things I need to tell you."

With a laugh Sidney caught his hand. "I understand. Let's say our goodbyes. I know just the place."

"This is the spot I had in mind." Sidney paused beside a large flat boulder.

She and Adam had returned to her cabin to release Picasso and Toulouse. Now the dog and cat ran ahead of them, pausing to sniff at animal tracks, happy to be free to run on this gloriously sunny day.

"Isn't this lovely?" They were standing beside a small pond located deep in the forest. The clearing was bathed in late-afternoon sunlight that spilled down through the branches of the trees in a benediction of golden rays.

"Yeah." Adam walked around, studying the spot from various angles. "Sit here." He helped her climb the boulder, before stepping back to study her through the viewfinder. "Stretch out your legs and lean back, resting your weight on your hands. Then look away from me and concentrate on the pond."

She did as he asked and saw a ripple of water indicating that something had moved. Intrigued, she forgot about the click of the camera as she strained to see what it was. A frog? A muskrat, perhaps? When nothing surfaced, she felt a keen sense of disappointment. She'd wanted to see something exotic swimming across the pond. The moment seemed to call for something extraordinary. Something that she could paint, if only in her mind.

Adam's voice brought her back. "I have some things I need to tell you, Sidney."

She looked up, but he was watching her through the lens of the camera, his voice sounding oddly detached. "Lean forward, bend your knees and wrap your arms around them while looking this way. Not at the camera, but beyond, as though watching something moving in the woods."

His sudden change of direction was disconcerting. Did he want to talk to her, or was this just a ruse to get the photographs he'd wanted?

With a series of yelps Picasso scared up a squirrel and was doing his imitation of a tree-climbing dog. Distracted, Sidney watched his antics, her expression changing quickly from dreamy to fascination to amusement, all of which were captured by Adam's camera.

"Perfect." Caught by her beauty he snapped several more shots before he was able to pull himself back. He struggled to keep his voice casual. "When we first met, I told you that I'd been injured."

She glanced over. "And were reluctant to tell me anything about it, as I recall."

He nodded. "It was wrong of me. I should have told you as soon as we met."

She could see that, despite the casual tone, his eyes were hard and his mouth grim. She felt a sudden frisson of alarm. "You can tell me whatever you need to, Adam. I'm willing to listen."

"My injuries were the result of a car bomb."

She looked up, eyes wide. "Now you're scaring me. Are you saying someone tried to kill you in your car?"

"Not me. A foreign ambassador who had attended a session of the United Nations. Both he and his assistant were killed. I was a witness to the incident. I'm told I was the only witness, since everyone else turned and ran at the moment of the explosion. Despite the fact that it happened in daylight, in the middle of New York City with all its crowds, the assassin managed to elude authorities. Ever since then, I've been targeted for murder."

"Murder?" The very word had her shuddering. Her throat went dry and it took her several seconds before she could find her voice. "But why aren't you in protective custody somewhere? Why are you here walking around if you're a target?"

"Protective custody didn't work. Even while I

was recovering in the hospital, the assassin was able to get close. After a consultation with the doctors and authorities, it was decided that a lighthouse in the middle of a wilderness would provide the perfect cover while I take the time to heal. Think about it. It's isolated from the outside world. Small enough that any stranger would be noted and reported.'' He lowered his camera and met her eyes. ''There are rules, of course, while trying to evade an assassin. I was made well aware of them. I understood them. I agreed to the terms. Unfortunately, I've managed to break most of them.''

''I don't understand.''

He lifted a hand to halt her questions before she could say more. ''The first and most important rule is to see that no innocents are caught up in the danger. I vowed, the first time I saw you here, to keep my distance, knowing that anyone who got close to me could become a target for a madman bent on silencing me. And then I proceeded to break that vow over and over. Today, when I met with your grandfather, I was reminded of the peril you could be facing because of my selfishness.''

Her head came up. Her eyes narrowed. ''You discussed this with Poppie?''

''His mind is sharp as a razor. He recognized me from news clippings he'd read about the case, and was naturally concerned for the safety of his granddaughter.''

"Naturally." If Adam were paying closer attention, he might have noted the thread of anger beneath that single word, which she uttered through clenched teeth.

"I agreed with him that I owed you the truth, so that you could make plans for your safety."

She brought her hands to her temples and rubbed. "This isn't at all what I'd expected you to tell me." She didn't add that she'd been agonizing about the fact that he might have a wife or significant other waiting for him in some faraway place. But this... this was almost more than she could take in. "Once again, it seems, my family was told all the facts about you before I could hear them."

"Not your family, Sidney. Just your grandfather. And only because, being a retired judge, he still keeps abreast of the more newsworthy cases."

She knew that to be true. Still, it rankled that he'd confided in her grandfather before confiding in her.

"You realize that this sounds like something out of a spy novel."

"It's not fiction, Sidney. It's real life. And until the assassin is captured and put away for good, you're in as much danger as I am. And for that, I want you to know that I'm truly sorry. It was never my intention to bring trouble to your doorstep."

Despite her best intentions, tears shimmered in her eyes. "You make it sound so final. As though we're both already dead."

''I never said that.'' Because he needed to touch her, he stepped closer and helped her down from the rock.

Her hands were cold, and he hated that he was the reason for it.

''I give you my word, Sidney, that I'll do everything in my power to keep you from being hurt. But it wasn't fair to keep this from you. You deserve to know just how much danger you're in because of me.''

He could see the fear and pain warring in her eyes, and knew that she was fighting real terror. And why not? What he'd just described to her was as far from her lifestyle as possible.

He released her hand and picked up the heavy duffel, slinging it over his shoulder. ''You'll want to get back. Maybe you'd like to pack.''

''Pack?'' She couldn't seem to keep up with the direction of his thoughts.

''I'm thinking that you'll probably want to go somewhere safe, like the Willows. I'm sure it would be comforting to be around your family for a while, at least until you've had time to let all these disturbing facts sink in.''

When he started away she stood back, watching the set of his shoulders, the firm stride. Like a soldier, she thought, about to head into battle.

But she was no soldier. She'd never faced the kind of danger Adam was talking about. The worst thing she'd ever had to deal with was the death of a loved one. She simply had no weapons with which to fight a professional assassin who had coldly killed, and would again.

He had rightly determined that she was afraid. In fact, she was absolutely terrified. And her first thought was to run as far and as fast as she could. But now, as she trailed slowly behind him, she was already arguing the wisdom of that reaction.

How could she even consider leaving her cabin, her independence, and moving back home with her family? For how long? Who was to say if this assassin would ever be found? If not, would she be willing to remain safely locked away for weeks, months, years?

It was a struggle to keep up with Adam's brisk steps. As they approached her cabin, Picasso and Toulouse were already there, eager to be the first ones inside. She stared at them, and then at her cabin, with a jumble of emotions. Fear. Anger. Hunger for things to remain the way they were.

She wanted her safe world back. Or at least the illusion of safety she'd harbored yesterday and the day before. But now that she knew about the dangers, how was she supposed to react?

Adam actually thought she ought to pack up and run away. But how could she leave the life she'd so painstakingly built for herself and go back to living with her family? Especially when she had no idea just how long she would have to be gone. It wasn't possible to pack away her dreams again, to put them into storage along with her life, while she waited for something that may or may not happen.

Adam paused at the door. "I'll help you pack."

Despite the fears that were tumbling around inside her mind, she gave a firm shake of her head. "No."

"Let me give you a hand, Sidney. It's the least I can do."

She lifted her chin. "You don't understand, Adam. I'm not leaving."

"Have you heard anything I said?"

She stood her ground. "I have. And I appreciate your honesty. For a man who treasures his privacy, it must have been difficult for you to share this with me. Of course, I realize you only did it to placate my grandfather. Now it's your turn to hear me. This is my home. I fought long and hard to make it mine, and I'm not about to give it up."

He swore under his breath and fought the urge to shake her. Instead, he curled his hands into fists at his sides and said through gritted teeth, "You don't have to give it up forever. Just leave until the authorities capture the man they're looking for. Then it'll be safe for you to return."

"How long has this man eluded capture? Weeks? Months? What makes you think he'll be found anytime soon? Would you have me put my life on hold indefinitely?"

"You can certainly continue to live your life while staying at the Willows."

"I love my family home. It's filled with happy memories. But *this* is my home now."

She turned the key in the lock and watched as her dog and cat raced inside ahead of her. On the threshold she turned to him, her eyes now free of tears, her face composed. She didn't invite him inside. In fact, the way she stood, barring the way, told him all too clearly that he wasn't welcome.

"Thank you for telling me the truth, Adam. I appreciate your honesty and your concern. Now it's time for you to go."

"You don't really expect me to just walk away and leave you here all alone."

"I was alone long before you came to Devil's Cove, Adam, and I've managed to survive. I'll survive long after you've gone back to your job at WNN. However much my grandfather may have bullied you into believing otherwise, you're not responsible for me."

"Packing up and going back to the Willows wasn't your grandfather's suggestion. It's mine. This isn't your fight. You have no defense against a hired killer. I'll sleep better knowing you're out of the line of fire."

"How nice for you, Adam. I'm sorry if my being here is going to cause you to lose sleep. But my life and how I choose to live it is no business of yours. Not now. Not ever.''

''Sidney...'' He had just opened his mouth to protest when the door was closed, loudly and firmly, in his face.

Chapter 10

Sidney stood just inside the door, listening as Adam gunned the engine and took off with tires spewing gravel along the trail that led away from her cabin.

"How dare you!" She stormed around the room, temper in full boil. "You come to my town, my woods, my little slice of paradise, and turn it upside down. And then you and Poppie cook up this scheme to keep me safe. Did you really think that by telling me I might be in danger that I would just pack up and leave? Do you think me such a coward that I need the comfort of my family to survive? I don't need you, Adam Morgan. So you can just go on your merry way for all I care."

Picasso and Toulouse lay by the hearth, waiting for the fire they'd come to expect. They weren't disappointed. Needing something to do, Sidney struggled under the weight of a huge log, positioning it on the grate before adding kindling, then holding a match to it until a fire was blazing.

Intrigued by her frantic activity, they began grooming themselves as she resumed her pacing. "Do he and Poppie actually think they can just pat me on the head and placate me?" She spooned food into the pet bowls and slammed them down by the door. The dog and cat, thinking it was a game, pounced on their food while she stormed to the kitchen, muttering, "There, there, little girl. Just go back home and live with your family, and don't worry your pretty little head about all this trouble I mentioned. You'll be safe, and the big bad wolf won't get you."

She filled the kettle and banged it on the stove. "Trudy can feed you, and Poppie can protect you, and Bert can soothe you. Isn't that enough? Oh, what's that? You want someone to love you, to respect you, to treat you like someone with a brain, as well?" Her tone changed to a snarl. "You want too much, little girl. Isn't it enough to be fed and protected and soothed? Nobody gets to have it all. But at least you'll be safe. And isn't that what you've always wanted? A nice, safe, dull life? Yes, that's it. That's what you deserve, while I'm out covering wars and doing my best to change the world.''

With her words vibrating around the empty cabin she sat down on the hearth and buried her face in her hands, sobbing quietly. Alarmed, the dog and cat circled her, trying in vain to offer comfort. But she was lost in her own misery and refused to let them close until, desperate, Picasso began to whine. When she lifted her head the dog put a paw on her lap, while Toulouse began to lick Sidney's hand.

Upset, she gathered them close and fought back fresh tears as panic began to set in. ''That's what I am, you know. Dull. Dull and ordinary. Living my dull, ordinary life.'' She sniffed. ''And how can an ordinary woman stay here alone? I'd be a fool to risk my safety with a madman on the prowl. But what if he's thousands of miles away by now? Do I leave all this and go back home, just because I'm afraid? Won't I be just as afraid at the Willows, knowing Adam is living out here, facing the threat alone? And for how long will I hide myself away? A week? A month? A year? When will I get over my fear?''

She closed her eyes against the pain. Her road to this place in her life had been such a long, hard, uphill battle. And now she was being asked to give it all up and start over, just to be certain she was safe.

Still, she didn't see any better solution to ease her

fears. For the truth was she was afraid. Desperately afraid. But knowing that her options were limited to staying or fleeing didn't make it any easier. She sniffed back tears, wishing she could call back her temper. Anger was infinitely better than this feeling of utter helplessness.

She glanced up at her studio, wondering how many art supplies would fit in her Land Rover.

"No." She stood, swallowing back her fear. She would not allow it to defeat her. "I'm not packing up and leaving."

Though she was weary beyond belief, she wondered if she would be able to sleep at all this night. It seemed useless to even bother undressing. Still, the thought of a long hot bath and some time spent in front of the fire seemed a better option than pacing and muttering.

Picasso's ears lifted and he raced to the door, tail wagging, body wriggling with excitement. Toulouse followed suit, standing at attention beside the door.

"What is it?" Suddenly alert, Sidney got to her feet and wiped furiously at her eyes.

"Sidney."

At the sound of Adam's fierce voice, she stormed across the room and shouted at the closed door, "Go away. You've done enough damage for one day."

He pounded the door with his fist, causing the dog and cat to start dancing around in circles. "I'm not leaving until you unlock this door."

"Fine. Just stand out there all night and freeze, for all I care." She turned away and paced to the kitchen, to lift the whistling kettle from the stove.

There was another loud knock on the door, and Adam's voice sounded as furious as she felt. "Open this door. We need to talk."

"You've said it all. There may or may not be a madman on the loose. I may or may not be in danger. But either way, since I'm such a helpless female, you and my grandfather think that I really ought to pack up and run. I don't believe there's anything left for you to say."

"Sidney." His tone was softer now. Not so much angry as sorry. "Please."

Sidney laid a hand on the door and pressed her forehead to the cold wood. "I can't, Adam. Can't you see that I'm trying to deal with this in my own way?"

"Yes. I can. Now just open the door."

She looked at the dog, staring hopefully at the door, tail beating a jungle rhythm on the floor. And then at her cat dancing circles and waiting anxiously for the door to open.

Their reactions were nothing compared with her heart, beating a wild tattoo in her chest. She hated that, even now, with hurt and anger bubbling inside, this man's mere presence could make her feel something more. Something wild and desperate and hopeful.

She turned the lock and opened the door just a crack. "Don't think this means—"

Before she could get the words out, Adam strode inside and grabbed her roughly by the upper arms, staring at her with such intensity, it had her pulse speeding up. "You've been crying."

She drew back, struggling for dignity. "I always cry when I'm afraid or mad."

"You've got every right to be both. I've managed, in a couple of weeks, to turn your safe world on its ear."

Safe. Dull. In her mind, those two words had come to mean something very similar.

Her chin came up in that infuriating way he'd come to recognize. "Yes, you have. Thank you very much."

While they stood toe-to-toe, the dog and cat danced eagerly around their ankles. Adam and Sidney took no notice.

Much to her horror, instead of bothering to reply, Adam hauled her roughly into his arms and kissed her until they were both breathless. When at last he lifted his head, she found herself struggling to fill her lungs.

He kept her close, his words muffled against her temple. "I'm so sorry, Sidney. Sorry for making such a mess of this. Sorry for confiding in your grandfather before you. Sorry for not telling you the truth the first time I realized what you were beginning to mean to me.''

''And just what *do* I mean to you?''

''More than I wanted.'' He held on tightly. ''If you won't pack up and go where it's safe, I've decided that I'll just have to stay here with you.''

''*You* decided?'' She pushed free of his arms. ''Just like that, *you* decided? What about what *I* want?''

His eyes narrowed on her. ''It's what you want, too.''

''How dare you presume—''

''Don't lie. Not to me. Not to yourself, Sidney.'' His words were a strangled snarl. ''If I wanted to, I could have you out of those clothes and into your bed inside of five minutes.''

''I think I'd have something to say about that.''

In reply he lowered his mouth to hers. The longer he lingered over her lips, the more a feeling of weakness seemed to spread through her limbs, until she wondered that she could still stand. Reflexively she wrapped her arms around his waist and held on tightly as she kissed him back.

When the kiss ended he lifted his head and regarded her through narrowed eyes. If his breath was a little ragged, and his throat far too dry, he chose to ignore it. ''Now try to tell me you wouldn't come willingly to bed with me.''

Her eyes frosted over, and then her tone. ''Was

there some point to that…experiment, other than your ego?''

''The point is, despite what you say, your kisses tell me something else. You want me here, Sidney.'' His tone lowered with passion. ''And the truth is, I want to be here with you.''

''I don't need you to protect me.''

''Maybe not. But I need to be here. Not for your sake, but for mine. I need to and I want to.'' His voice became a fierce, impassioned whisper. ''Let me stay, Sidney.''

''Because you feel responsible for me now.''

''Because I want, more than anything in this world, to be here with you.'' He took in a breath, fighting to remain calm. ''I told your grandmother that I couldn't be what you want. And that's probably true. But true or not, I need to be here with you.''

''And just what is it you think I want?''

''You want what your grandparents have. What your parents had. What your sisters have found.''

''What's wrong with wanting that?''

''Nothing. That's the natural order of things. A man, a woman and a vow to remain together for a lifetime. That's exactly what you deserve. But I'm not the guy who can give it to you.''

''Of course not.'' Her voice was pure sarcasm. ''Why would a man who's been all over the world want to spend time here with me?''

"Stop putting yourself down. I love being here with you. But I don't know how I'll feel a few weeks from now, a few months from now, let alone years. This is all new to me. And I'm not going to lie just to get you into bed."

"I suppose I should thank you for your honesty."

"I don't want your thanks." He started to reach for her, then seemed to think better about it. "I was sorely tempted to tell you what you wanted to hear, just to satisfy my own needs. If you weren't so special…" He shook his head. "I don't know what's come over me. I'm not the hero type. But you…you deserve all the happiness in the world. Certainly more happiness than I can offer you."

"I'll be the judge of what I want."

At her tone he lifted his head. "All right. I've had my say. Now it's your turn. Go ahead, Sidney. Hit me with your best shot. I deserve it."

She clutched her hands together tightly at her waist, as though holding herself together by sheer willpower. "You seem to know me very well. It's true that I want all the things you said. And someday I'll have them. But right now, I want you to stay the night, Adam."

If the earth had opened up and swallowed him, he wouldn't have been more surprised. His voice was rougher than he intended. "Even after everything I said?"

She nodded. "Maybe I was hoping for a promise

of a lifetime together. But if I've learned anything in this life, it's that promises, no matter how heartfelt, can't always be kept. I won't hold you when you're ready to move on. But for whatever time we have left, I'd like to spend it together.''

He was looking at her as though he couldn't believe what he'd heard. With a quick shake of his head he closed a hand over her wrist. ''Sidney.'' His voice was little more than a hoarse whisper. He looked down at her hand, then into her eyes. ''What you're offering is everything I've ever wanted. But don't you understand that I'm trying to do the right thing?''

''Yes. And that just makes me...want you more.'' She hated the fact that he could hear the tremor in her voice, and see the way her eyes were filling. ''Stay the night, Adam. But not because you're afraid of leaving me alone. Stay because you want to be with me. And if you want to leave in the morning, I promise I won't hold you.''

With a sigh of impatience he framed her face with his hands, as though peering deep into her soul, before pressing his lips to the corner of her eye.

At the first salty taste of her tears he knew he was lost. In one swift motion his arms were around her, dragging her close, while his mouth covered hers in a kiss so hot, so hungry, she was nearly consumed by it.

His hand fisted in her hair as he drank her in like

a man starved for the taste of her. The hand at her
shoulder tightened, and she could feel the tension
throbbing through him. As he deepened the kiss it
was neither soft nor easy as the others had been, but
rough, needy. She found the fact that he was fighting
for control deeply arousing. She returned his kisses
with a passion that startled her. Now that she'd
opened herself up to him, there seemed no way to
stop the needs that rushed to the surface. The need
to have his hands on her until she trembled. The
need to have his mouth moving over hers until they
devoured each other. The need to put aside all the
restrictions she'd set on herself and simply indulge
her passions until she was sated.

How long? she wondered, as the kiss spun on and
on until her blood ran hot from it. How long had
she forced herself to live by a strict code of conduct?
To pretend that nothing mattered in life except her
art? And now, suddenly, her carefully laid plans
were tumbling wildly out of control. All because of
this man, and the need to be with him. To have him
with her.

"Understand," she whispered. "The choice is
mine. The decision mine."

Her heart was beating so wildly in her chest, she
feared it might simply explode. A wild, primal beat
that had the blood throbbing in her temples.

Even while these emotions thrilled her, they
frightened her. There was a darkness in Adam, a

taste of danger she'd never before experienced. Was that what set him apart from other men? That edge of excitement? His willingness to face the unknown? The sense that he'd seen things, done things, that she could only imagine?

He ran hot, wet kisses down her throat and heard her moan with pleasure. Suddenly all thought was wiped from her mind as she arched her neck to give him easier access.

He sighed in frustration when he encountered the neckline of her sweater. Before she could remove it he caught it by the hem and tore it over her head, then tossed it aside.

All he could do was stare as he held her a little away.

Desire slammed into him, and he fought to bank it. "You're so tiny. So delicate. So perfect." His words were little more than a ragged whisper as he studied the soft curves, barely covered by a hint of lace, and the narrow waist, nipped by the waistband of her skirt. "I'm afraid I'll hurt you."

"I can't change the fact that I'm small." She pressed a finger to his lips. "But I won't break, Adam. Touch me. I need you to touch me."

He did. And felt her tremble. When he cupped her breasts in his hands and followed with his lips, he felt a series of shudders ripple through her. Annoyed with even the simplest barrier between them, he tugged aside the wisp of lace, then did the same with her ankle-length skirt and panty hose. And then his hands were on her, and his mouth, that incredibly clever mouth, was moving over her relentlessly until she nearly wept with pleasure.

Her body was so delicate. All soft curves and tiny waist. Flesh as pale as milk. But her size was deceptive. There was strength here. In the eyes that stayed steady on his, despite whatever fears she might have harbored. In the hands that firmly tugged his shirt from his waistband and fumbled with the buttons.

At last she managed to slide it away from his shoulders. Then she was free to touch him as he was touching her.

This was what she'd wanted. Only this.

She loved the feel of those hard, corded muscles beneath her hands. She could feel them bunch and tighten with each touch. Those strong artist's fingers moved along the flat planes of his stomach, then upward across his hair-roughened chest. She heard him suck in a breath and it only made her bolder. Her fingertips encountered the long ridge of scar that ran from his chest to his shoulder and down his arm. She thought of the pain he'd endured and the strength he'd needed to survive, and her heart filled with a new and even greater emotion.

Without thinking she pressed her lips to the spot, causing his breath to back up in his lungs and his heart to thunder. For Sidney it was a heady feeling to know that it was her touch that had caused such a reaction.

The feel of her hands, her lips on his flesh, was the sweetest torture. The thought of taking her now, hard and fast, had the blood pounding in his temples.

Instead, he caught her by the upper arms and held her apart from him.

Misreading his intentions, she motioned toward the other room. "My bedroom..."

He gave a sound that might have been a laugh or a moan of frustration. "Too far."

"But it's only..."

He dragged her close and savaged her mouth, cutting off whatever else she'd been about to say. Then his hands were on her, rough with impatience, touching her everywhere. He trailed his lips over her body, pausing to taste, to nibble, until she couldn't seem to find enough breath to fill her lungs.

As he pleasured her and himself, the air around them seemed to thicken until each breath they took became an effort. Their bodies were soon slick with sheen.

He pushed her back against the wall and found her hot and wet. She was wonderful to watch as he drove her to the first peak. He saw her eyes widen, the pupils darken with passion. She tried to speak his name. Before she could, he covered her mouth with his and kissed her until they were both gasping.

Her legs were trembling, and she feared they

could no longer hold her. As if sensing her need he caught her hands and lowered her to the floor. Though the sofa was just steps away, even that was too far now. Caught in the blinding heat of passion, all they could do was cling as they took each other into the very heart of the fire.

"Sidney." He framed her face with his hands, staring into her eyes with an intensity that had her heart thundering. "My sweet, beautiful Sidney. You're so much more than I deserve." And still, knowing that, he had a desperate need to possess her, to make her his alone. He continued to kiss, to caress, to drive her closer and closer to the edge. It was deeply arousing to cause her to lose all control, and to know that he was the reason.

She sighed and moved in his arms, her eyes steady on his, all her focus on him. At this moment he was the center of her universe. The world outside this room no longer mattered. The wind sighing in the trees couldn't match the sob that caught in her throat at he moved over her, kissing her, touching her. The chill air of the cabin couldn't cool her heated flesh. The ticking of the clock on the mantel couldn't match the erratic beat of her out-of-control pulse.

When she dragged his face down for one more slow, drugging kiss, he found himself slipping beyond reason.

He'd fought so hard for control. He'd wanted to

take her gently, as she deserved. But now the needs inside him were struggling like wild beasts to break free, and he was helpless to hold them at bay.

His mouth savaged hers. His hands dug into her hair, pulling her head back fiercely so that he could look into her eyes as he entered her. For one brief moment he went perfectly still, shocked that he could be so rough with one who deserved better.

"Adam. Oh, yes, Adam." With her body arching into his, she wrapped herself around him and drew him in deeper.

He was lost. He could no longer deny the need that was all-consuming.

He felt his entire body and soul straining toward release, and marveled at her strength as she kept pace. Her nails scraped his flesh. Her eyes opened, staring into his as she began to move with him, climb with him.

They were tossed into the foaming, churning waters of a storm-tossed lake, and still they continued to move. Arms clinging. Lungs straining. Hearts racing as they hurtled through space, shattering into millions of tiny pieces before drifting on a gentle current toward a distant light.

Chapter 11

"That was…" Words failed her, and Sidney felt her throat clog with unshed tears.

"Incredible." He lifted a finger to her mouth. Traced the outline of her lips, still warm and moist from his kisses. "And so are you."

Her mouth curved into a smile. "You're not half-bad, either."

"Gee, thanks." He chuckled, and the warmth of it spread through her, leaving her feeling incredibly lighthearted.

He waited for his world to settle. When it did, he managed to lift his weight from her, rolling to one side and drawing her into the circle of his arms.

He played with a strand of her hair. "The first

time I saw you, all I could see was this.'' He lifted a handful of hair and watched as the silken strands sifted through his fingers. ''The color of autumn leaves. And then I saw your face, and for a minute I was robbed of speech.'' He stared into her eyes. ''Do you have any idea how beautiful you are?''

''Adam, don't tease.'' She could feel the heat rushing to her cheeks.

He shook his head. ''You really don't know, do you?'' Before she could protest, he traced the outline of her eyebrow, her cheek, her chin. ''Let me tell you what I see when I look at you, Sidney.'' He took her hand in his and brought it to his mouth, pressing a kiss to the palm. ''You're so small, so delicate looking. But I see such strength in you. You can do anything you choose. And what you choose is a life apart from others, not because you shun people, but rather because you need to avoid distractions in order to feed your art.''

Her eyes widened. ''It's true. How did you know?''

''Because we're soul mates.'' He pressed a kiss to her eyelid. ''And these eyes. Others only see eyes so green, they put the waters of Lake Michigan to shame. But I see old pain in their depths, along with honesty. Integrity.''

He'd seen her pain. The truth of that statement pierced her heart.

He brushed his lips over her forehead, the curve

of her cheek. "Your skin is so flawless, makeup would be an insult. And this mouth." He covered it with his own and murmured, "I love kissing your mouth, Sidney. I'll never have enough of it. Or of you."

On a sigh he took the kiss deeper, then deeper still. And then there were no more words needed between them as he showed her, with soft sighs and tender touches, all the things that he was feeling.

At a movement beside her, Sidney stirred. "Did I fall asleep?"

"Only for a few minutes." Adam gathered her into his arms and carried her to the sofa. "You're cold. I'll get a fire going."

She seemed surprised to discover that she'd been lying naked beside him, with only their clothing and a rug to cushion them.

He settled her on the sofa and wrapped her in an afghan before crossing the room to stir the coals on the hearth and add a log. Instead of returning to her side he rummaged in the refrigerator. A short time later he set two mugs of hot chocolate on the coffee table and handed one to her before sitting down beside her.

She offered him part of the afghan, draping it around his shoulders. "I'm not accustomed to being waited on."

He shot her a grin. "I can see that. You're used to doing things for yourself."

"Do you think there's something wrong with that?"

He shook his head. "Not at all. It's been my rule of thumb for most of my life." He gave her a sideways glance. "We're a lot alike, Sidney. Loners, content with our own company. Workaholics, with no sense of time or place."

She smiled. "I hadn't thought of that. And here I was thinking how different we are."

"In what way?"

"You're at home anyplace in the world. I'm only happy when I'm here in Devil's Cove. You willingly put yourself in harm's way for the sake of your job. I'm the biggest coward in the world. I can't imagine having the courage to face down danger, not just once but over and over again."

"You're talking about guns and bombs and land mines. But what about the perils of everyday life? There are different degrees of danger, Sidney. You never know how much courage you have until you're called upon to face a challenge."

She was already shaking her head. "My life here in Devil's Cove seems like a piece of cake next to yours. I'll take the dangers of living here over wars and rebel uprisings in some faraway country any day."

He took her empty mug from her hand and set it

down beside his before gathering her into his arms. Against her lips he muttered, "Enough talk about how alike or different we are. Here's one thing we can absolutely agree on."

Whatever she'd been about to say was gone from her mind in an instant. With one kiss, one touch, she welcomed the tug of sexual desire as she lost herself in the pleasure he offered.

Sidney lay very still, wondering for a moment where she was. Then it came rushing back to her. The night of loving, the whispered words of endearment, the passion, the tenderness.

Sometime during the night she and Adam had tired of their cramped quarters on the sofa and had run, holding hands and laughing like loons, to her bedroom. Without bothering to turn on a light, using just the faint glow of the fireplace, they'd tumbled into bed. Afterward, there had been little time for words. Lost in the wonder of their newly discovered passion, they'd been insatiable.

Sidney yawned and stretched, then went very still as she realized she was alone in bed. She fought a wave of disappointment, until she heard the outer door open and close and heard Adam's deep voice. In reply, the cabin was filled with Picasso's yelp of pleasure and Toulouse's answering meow.

Moments later the bedroom door opened and Adam stepped in, carrying a tray.

"Oh, Adam." Sidney sat up, shoving a tangle of hair from her eyes. "Is that coffee I smell?"

"It is. I was hoping you were awake." He set the tray on the night table and settled himself on the edge of the bed before covering her mouth with his. Though he kept the kiss light, they both felt the familiar jolt and moved apart reluctantly.

"What's this?" He grinned at the way she was holding the sheets almost to her chin. "It's a little late for modesty, don't you think?"

She laughed. "I suppose so. But I don't see you walking around in your birthday suit."

"That's because it was cold when I woke up. I pulled on my shirt and pants for warmth until I could get the fire going. Besides, one of us has to be sensible. Poor Picasso and Toulouse were desperate to get outside for a morning run. And while I was up, I decided to make breakfast."

She glanced at the tray. "Careful. I may start to like being pampered."

"I'm not being entirely selfless." He wiggled his eyebrows and lowered his voice to a mock villain's purr. "I'm hoping you'll be so grateful, you'll throw yourself into my arms and let me have my way with you."

She lowered her head and batted her eyelashes. "Would you like my gratitude before I eat, or after?"

"I'll wait until you're fed, so you have more stamina."

"A very smart man."

"I do my best." He climbed into bed beside her, then settled the tray between them.

As Sidney helped herself to scrambled eggs and bit into cinnamon toast, she couldn't hold back her little sigh of approval. "I believe you've just earned a very special debt of gratitude, Mr. Morgan."

His grin was quick and dangerous. "Eat faster, Ms. Brennan. I'm not sure I can wait much longer to see what you have in mind."

After several more bites, their food was forgotten as they fell laughing into each other's arms. Within minutes the laughter had been replaced with ragged breathing and hot, hungry kisses as they took each other on another breathless roller-coaster ride.

Adam opened the bedroom drapes and peered out at the leaden sky. "Looks like rain."

Sidney sat back against the pillows, feeling pleasantly sated. She couldn't recall the last time she'd enjoyed such a lazy morning. "Then I guess I won't be working outside today."

"Me, either." He turned to her with a wicked grin. "But I'm sure we can find something entertaining to do indoors."

"You're incorrigible." She was laughing as he

moved around her room, seeing it in the light for the first time.

It was nearly as big as the rest of the cabin combined, with a stone fireplace dominating one wall. The furniture was simple. Besides the bed there was a small sofa and footstool positioned near the fire, and an antique desk and chair beneath one large window.

Adam studied the framed picture that stood on the mantel and carefully schooled his features before turning to her. "Is this a wedding photograph?"

Her gaze flew to the picture and then to his face. "Actually, it's an almost wedding photo."

"Almost?" He picked it up to study it closer. It was then that he realized the man in the tuxedo and the very young Sidney in her wedding gown were seated on a bed.

She spoke slowly, haltingly, as though measuring each word for fear of choking on it. "His name is Curt Mayhue. We met in college and were instantly attracted. I was a student and he was revered as the finest, and youngest, art instructor on campus. When we learned that his health was seriously deteriorating, we decided to move ahead quickly with our decision to marry and follow our dreams, foolishly believing, I suppose, that love would conquer all and be enough to give us our happy ending."

He heard the thread of pain beneath the words. "He didn't rally?"

She swallowed hard. "Curt died before we could actually speak our vows."

"Oh, baby." He set aside the picture and crossed to her. Gathering her close he pressed his mouth to her temple. "I can imagine how it hurt."

She couldn't hide the tears. They spilled silently down her cheeks. "I've never talked about it out loud before."

"Not even to your family?"

She shook her head. "At first it was too painful. And then, when I returned to Devil's Cove, we all tiptoed around it, afraid of opening up old wounds."

He held her as gently as fragile glass, allowing her to weep against his chest. When at last she took a long, deep sigh, he held her a little away. "You mentioned a return to Devil's Cove. Is that after you lived in Tuscany?"

She nodded. "I tried to live out the dreams we'd planned together, until I realized they wouldn't work for me. So I came home to pursue my own."

He framed her face and brushed soft kisses over her eyes, her nose, her lips. "Has anyone told you what a smart woman you are?"

"Yeah." She drew in a shuddering breath. "That's me. Smart Sidney Brennan, who has to learn everything the hard way."

"And what have you learned about Sidney Brennan?"

She thought a minute before saying haltingly,

"That she can be alone and like it. That immersing herself in her work can make time pass, even if it sometimes moves at the pace of a snail." Sidney took a deep breath and spoke quickly, before she could lose her nerve. "That she can have her heart broken and survive."

"You're not only gorgeous and talented, Sidney Brennan, but also exceptionally smart." He kept his hands on either side of her face as he lowered his mouth to hers. "Maybe things learned the hard way are remembered longest. I know I'll never forget this night. Or the woman I spent it with."

This time he drew out the kiss until they were both struggling for breath.

"I think," he muttered thickly, "we're about to skip lunch and dinner completely and go right to dessert."

"You don't talk about your family, Adam." Sidney looked at their linked hands, enjoying the pleasant glow from their lovemaking. "Do you have any?"

He nodded. "A kid sister. She's married, living in Georgia with her husband and three kids now."

"Your parents?"

"My dad died when I was ten. My mother passed away six years ago. I lived with her for a couple of years after my dad's death, until she decided that I needed a father figure and sent me to live with my uncle, my father's brother.''

"Did you mind?"

"Not really. I felt closer to him than I did to the man my mom married shortly after that. When they sold the family house in Florida, nothing ever seemed like home again.''

Sidney tried to imagine being without a home. It would be like finding herself without a port in a storm. Without a safe refuge from the slings and arrows of life. It was simply impossible to contemplate.

"Is that why you took a job that sends you all over the world?''

"Could be. I've never really thought about it. I've always been driven to see new places, try new things. But I suppose it's easier for someone like me, who's not constantly yearning for something safe and familiar back home.'' Because old habits were hard to break, he switched the topic of conversation as easily as he would a light switch. "Tell me about your days as an art student.''

Sidney sighed. "Those were glorious days. I was finally beginning to see the long road toward my goal.''

"You always knew you'd be an artist?''

She nodded. "It's all I'd ever wanted. My family encouraged me. And then, with Curt's prodding, I started to blend my goals with his.'' She found it so liberating to finally be able to speak of those days, and her life with Curt. After holding it all inside for so long, the words came tumbling out. "I was young and impressionable. He was my mentor, my teacher, as well as the first real love of my life, and I was overwhelmed, not only by his attention but by his amazing talent."

"Pretty heady stuff for a college student."

"It was." She found herself relieved that Adam understood. "It all happened so quickly, there was never time to sort it out. And then, just as quickly, Curt was gone, and I was alone before I'd even had a chance to live as his wife. I was grieving, but not as a widow. I was still Sidney Brennan, aspiring artist, with her whole life ahead of her. And yet, I felt as though I had nothing left to look forward to. Gradually I realized that you don't get over something like that. You just move on."

"A hard lesson." He lifted her hand to his mouth. "And yet you survived."

She traced a fingertip along the scar that ran in a jagged line across his shoulder and down his torso. "We're both survivors. This had to be a nightmare."

He attempted to shrug it off. "At least I lived. The ambassador and his assistant weren't as lucky."

"Can you tell me about it?"

He was silent for so long, Sidney thought he might refuse to speak of it.

"Understand, some of it is still a blur. There are bits and pieces missing from my memory." He took a breath, as though gathering his recollection. "I wasn't supposed to be there. Another photographer for WNN was supposed to be covering the arrival of the ambassador, but at the last minute he called in sick, and since I was in New York anyway, I dashed across town to cover it. I was just turning away after videotaping their departure from the UN when the car bomb exploded. It was so powerful, I could feel the street shuddering. I knew I ought to get as far away, and quickly, as I could. Everyone else was smart enough to do just that. But my mind had gone into autopilot, and instead of running, I stayed and snapped as many photos as I could until a second explosion erupted. That time, I wasn't so lucky. I was hit by the debris, and the next thing I knew I was being rushed by ambulance to a hospital." He gave a dry laugh. "I was still snapping pictures until I lost consciousness."

"Oh, Adam. How terrifying." Sidney pressed a kiss to the scar. "I can't bear to think about the pain you must have suffered."

"It's over, Sidney. At least most of it." He drew her into the circle of his arms. "And to think I fought against taking sick leave. I'd convinced myself that spending time in Devil's Cove would drive me around the bend." He kissed her, slow and deep. Against her lips he whispered, "Now it's the beautiful woman in my arms who's sending me around the bend.''

She sighed. ''I'm happy to oblige. Just doing my part to assist in your therapy.'' Her sigh turned into a little moan of pleasure as he moved his mouth lower, then lower still.

Then there were no more words between them as they slipped away to another world.

''What are you painting?'' Adam was standing in the center of the room, his camera focused on Sidney, who was above him in the loft.

In the background, her grandmother's album was playing. The score from *Camelot*. When he'd first heard the old, unfamiliar songs, he'd thought them far too sugary. Now, as the words played softly, he found himself humming along. It was a grand and heartbreakingly sad and complex love story.

''A hawk.'' She stood at her easel, palette in hand, mixing paints and dabbing them on the canvas. She was dressed in a pair of faded denims and a candy-striped shirt that had seen better days. Her hair hung long and loose to her waist. Her head was tipped up, her eyes focused on the hawk gliding in slow, even circles just above the treetops visible outside the skylights.

''You're a photographer's dream, Sidney.''

She glanced down at him absently. ''What does that mean?''

''Nothing. Go on about your business, and I'll do the same.'' He studied her through the viewfinder, and waited for her to return her attention to the canvas.

It didn't matter what she wore, or how she fixed her hair, or in this case, didn't fix it. Whether dressed in elegant clothes, as she'd been for her family's Sunday brunch, or in today's paint-spattered work clothes, she was the image of classic beauty. It was simply impossible for her to look anything but spectacular in a photograph. Which was why he continued snapping until he'd completed another roll of film. He was driven to capture her in all her many moods, just as the song expressed. How could he leave her in spring, summer, winter or fall, when each of them seemed to bring out another hidden facet of her beauty?

He set aside his camera and stowed the used film in his duffel. A glance at his watch had him looking out the window in surprise. Where had the day gone? He couldn't remember the last time he'd been so distracted that an entire day had come and gone without a desire to leave the confines of four walls.

Seeing that Sidney was still absorbed in her canvas, he walked to the kitchen and began checking out something to fix for dinner.

An hour later, after cleaning her brushes in the shed out back, Sidney stepped inside the cabin and breathed deeply. ''What is that wonderful smell?''

"I'm roasting a chicken with sage dressing."

"You're..." A wide smile curved her lips. "You're going to feed me again?"

"I love feeding you." Adam caught her hands.

"Only because you like the way I show my gratitude."

"There is that." He drew her close and brushed a kiss over her lips. "If you'd like to do so now, I believe we have time. The chicken needs at least another hour."

"Bless that chicken." She was laughing as she led the way to her bedroom.

In the doorway she paused. The bed linens had been turned down invitingly. A cozy fire burned on the grate.

She turned to Adam, standing behind her, who'd been watching her reaction. Without a word she went to him.

As she reached for the buttons of her shirt he shook his head and lifted his hands to hers. "Let me."

He took his time undressing her, and let her do the same with him. Together they slipped into bed. With long, unhurried kisses they took each other, feeling the need gradually build from heat to inferno. Like two old lovers who had all the time in the world, they drew out each pleasure, lingered over each kiss, each touch, until at last they came together, warmed not only by the fire that blazed on the hearth, but also by the flame that burned hot and bright in their hearts.

When at last they lay, calm and settled, he touched a finger to her cheek. "Would you like to sleep awhile?"

She shook her head. "I'm too happy to sleep. I just want to lie here with you, Adam."

He lay with his hand under his head, the other hand holding hers, fingers linked, staring into the flames. His attention was caught by the framed picture on the mantel.

Almost married.

He'd found the phrase odd when Sidney had first said it. Now he had to admit to himself that it was exactly right. It was what he was feeling with her now.

He'd always told himself that marriage was for ordinary men with ordinary jobs. A man who made his living chronicling life's misery in the far corners of the world had no right to an ordinary man's dreams and desires.

But at least for this day, in this cabin with Sidney, he was feeling as close to married as he'd ever been.

Not that he was fooling himself. He had no right to subject a woman as special as Sidney to the kind of worry his lifestyle would create. Still, it was pleasant, just for this day and night, to live out the fantasy.

The realities of his life, he thought with sudden

clarity, were bound to come charging back all too soon. Wasn't that why he'd come back to her? To assure himself that he would do everything in his power to keep her safe? Or were there other reasons, as well? Reasons he didn't care to probe too deeply?

They both dozed, while the music of Camelot played softly in the other room.

An hour later, with Picasso and Toulouse attacking their pet dishes, Sidney and Adam sat on the sofa in front of the fire and enjoyed their dinner.

After the first bite, Sidney sighed. "I want this recipe."

He sipped a cold beer. "I'll write it down for you. Or you could make it easy on yourself by just keeping me around so I could fix it for you."

"Deal." Sidney laughed easily. "What did you and Bert talk about on your walk after brunch?"

"You, mostly."

"What did you say about me?"

"That I'm crazy about you."

Sidney's jaw dropped. "You told my grandmother that?"

He chuckled and leaned over to brush a kiss over her lips. "You can close your mouth now, Sidney. It's not some earthshaking announcement. She asked how I felt about you and I told her."

"But you never even told me."

"I'm telling you now."

"So you are." She huffed out a breath and

seemed to consider for a moment. "I seem to hear everything last, after you've told my family."

"Maybe I like them better than you."

That had her laughing out loud as she began gathering up the dishes and carrying them to the kitchen. He walked up behind her and wrapped his arms around her waist, pressing his lips to the nape of her neck. "I was thinking we could do those dishes later."

She glanced at the raindrops streaking the windows. "It's too wet to walk off our meal."

"Maybe I have something better in mind than a walk."

"Glutton." She was laughing as he caught her hand and led her toward the bedroom.

Chapter 12

"Snowflakes." Adam turned on his windshield wipers. "Isn't it too early for snow?"

Sidney fastened her seat belt. "Anybody who lives in Northern Michigan will tell you it's never too early for snow, unless it's the Fourth of July."

Adam found himself laughing.

"But I don't think it'll stick. The ground is too wet and too warm yet. Give it a couple more weeks, though, and it'll start to pile up." She stared out at the red-and-gold shower of leaves drifting past them on a cold blast of wind. "I've always loved the first snowfall of the year, when you wake up and everything is covered in a soft, white blanket."

"I'll take your word for it." He grinned at her.

"Which reminds me. As long as I'm picking up clean clothes at the lighthouse, I'll grab a parka, too." Thinking about snow had Adam turning up the heat.

"And as long as we're going into town afterward, I'll need to pick up some art supplies."

"Amazing what a day off routine can do." Adam shot her a smile. "I feel like I could walk a couple of miles through the woods without even breaking a sweat."

"Good. Maybe later on we could go hiking. I feel like I need to do something to work off all that food you've been fixing."

"Don't worry." He shot her a wicked grin. "I'm sure we can find a way to work off those excess calories."

"Oh, I'm sure we can. But once in a while it wouldn't hurt to change our routine."

"Routine? A few hours in my arms, and already I've become routine."

He turned the Jeep off the road and onto the lane that led to the lighthouse. "You can pick up your art supplies while I'm getting mauled by Marcella The Dominatrix."

"Watch it. I might decide to tell her what you've been calling her behind her back."

"Ouch." He rubbed his shoulder. "If she's rough now, just think what she'd do to me if she really wanted to give me a workout."

They shared another laugh. It occurred to Adam that he'd laughed more in the past day than he had in years.

"Actually," Sidney added. "My sister Emily says Marcella is just about the best physical therapist in the business."

"Is that what they're calling female wrestlers this year?"

They were still laughing as they pulled up to the lighthouse. Adam walked around and held the door, then took Sidney's hand in his as they walked together to the front door.

Inside he left her in the main room, while he went upstairs to his bedroom to pack a few things in his duffel. A short time later he sauntered down the stairs. "Before we go, I'll show you my darkroom."

She couldn't help chuckling. "If we hadn't just spent a great deal of time in bed, I'd think you were trying to seduce me."

"What makes you think I'm not?" He led the way to the small utility room and pushed open the door. Inside he flicked on a light.

Sidney stared around at the bottles of chemicals and assorted trays. "Oh, Adam, this is perfect. Won't it be satisfying to be able to develop your own film?"

"Definitely. Now that I have what I need, I figure I'll get started on that in the next couple of days.

It'll be a full-time job for awhile, since I've accumulated so many rolls of film.''

He was about to leave when he suddenly paused and bent to pick up a photograph from the floor. It was one of those he'd taken of Sidney by the shore. After studying it, he opened a manila folder and glanced at the other photos inside.

His tone hardened. "Someone was here, going through my things."

"How can you be certain?"

He turned the folder over. "I left this lying faceup. This photo was on the bottom of the stack."

"Why would someone want to look through a stack of photographs?"

"I don't know. But I intend to find out." He motioned toward the door and handed her the keys. "Lock yourself inside the Jeep and start the engine."

"What about you?"

"I'm going to check this place room by room."

"But what if the intruder is still here?"

His eyes were icy chips. "I don't have time for questions now, Sidney. But I need to know you're safe. Go. Now."

She ran outside to the Jeep and did as he'd ordered, then peered around nervously, afraid that at any moment she would hear the sound of gunfire. Forcing slow, deep breaths, she lectured herself on the need to remain calm. Calm. Her calm, orderly life had suddenly taken a turn she didn't like.

Inside, Adam made a thorough tour of the rooms, opening cabinets and closets and cupboards before climbing the light tower all the way to the dome. When he was satisfied that no one was hiding inside, he hurried from the lighthouse, holding a cell phone to his ear. As he settled into the Jeep for the ride to Devil's Cove, Sidney listened in silence as Adam spoke in rapid-fire tones to someone on the other end of the line.

"No footprints outside that were obvious, and no sign of forced entry. Except for the photograph in the darkroom, nothing else seemed out of place. And I didn't see any sign of destruction, but you might want to bring along someone from the historical society to take a look, just in case the intruder targeted something of value that I wouldn't know about."

He glanced at his watch. His tones were clipped. "If that's the way you want it, and you have a passkey, I can manage to stay away as long as you'd like. I was on my way to an appointment with my physical therapist when I discovered this breach. I'll go ahead and keep my appointment as though nothing has changed. I'd feel a whole lot better knowing that someone from the historical society has done a thorough check of their artifacts."

After setting aside his cell phone, he turned to Sidney. "Looks like we won't have to hurry home.

The authorities have Mrs. Maddox on the case. Do you know her?''

"The president of the historical society." Sidney peered around, certain that at any minute a car would shoot out of the cover of thick trees to block their path. "Mrs. Maddox is a retired school teacher who served with Bert for years at Devil's Cove High School. She'll relish the chance to play detective. But only as long as she knows there are real detectives along to see to her safety."

"She'll be safe. The Federal authorities assigned to the case will be with her. I'll feel a lot better knowing someone is going to check for any missing items owned by the historical society."

"What if nothing's missing?"

He shrugged. "Then we'll know it wasn't someone wanting to steal a piece of Michigan's history."

Despite his flippant remark, Adam had to nudge aside the nagging worry that it looked as though his idyll in this sleepy little town was about to come to a dramatic end.

He drove slowly through town and pulled up to the clinic. "Want to go inside the torture chamber with me?"

She linked her hand with his, needing to feel a connection with him, and marveled that even now, with this threat hanging over his head, he could keep things light. "I wouldn't miss it."

Inside Sidney took a seat while Adam pressed a

buzzer. Within minutes the inner door was opened, and Marcella Trowbridge was greeting them with a smile.

"I see you brought reinforcements." She smiled at Sidney. "Your sister tells me you're small but mighty, but I'm not sure you'd like to go up against me. I'm tougher than I look."

Despite the danger that minutes earlier had her looking over her shoulder in fear, Sidney found herself laughing along with this friendly young woman. "Not likely, Marcella. Your reputation precedes you. By the way, I hear congratulations are in order."

The young woman actually blushed. "Who'd have thought I'd find the love of my life where I least expected it?"

"Isn't that what they always say?"

"Uh-huh." Marcella turned to Adam. "Time's a-wasting. You'd better step into my office and strip." She gave a low chuckle as she nudged him in the ribs. "I love saying that to my clients."

When Sidney didn't follow, the therapist paused. "You coming in to watch the torture?"

Sidney shook her head. "I'm afraid you two will have to arm wrestle alone. I'm off to talk art supplies with Skeeter Hilton." She realized that she was actually looking forward to doing something normal, to keep her mind off the fear that was hovering over them like a dark cloud.

"A wise decision." Marcella winked. "Actually, what we do here isn't a pretty sight."

When Sidney was gone, Adam removed his shirt and took a seat on the stool Marcella indicated.

For the next half hour he followed her directions, working the damaged arm and shoulder in a series of movements that had him gritting his teeth in pain and frustration.

As always, Marcella kept up a steady teasing banter to keep his mind off his discomfort. Because Adam understood what she was doing, he played along, catching the gibes she tossed his way and throwing them right back at her.

"Good work," she said at one point, as sweat beaded on his forehead and began streaking down the sides of his face.

"Gee, thanks, Attila, I'm so glad you approve."

"Repeat after me," she deadpanned. "I love pain. Pain is my friend."

"Yeah, this is right up there as one of my all-time favorite pastimes. Right along with getting a tattoo or having various parts of my body pierced."

"Okay." She waited until he'd finished several repetitions of the exercise. "You can stop for a minute and relax."

Adam did as he was told. As Marcella began kneading the muscle of his shoulder she casually asked, "Oh, I almost forgot. Did your friend have any trouble finding you?"

"My friend?"

She slowly lifted his arm, had him hold it, then helped him lower it to his side. "I didn't get his name, but he said you and he worked together for WNN in the Middle East. He stopped by here—" she paused to consider "—either yesterday or the day before that. I've been so busy, I'm not sure of the day. But he said he knew you were getting therapy, and since this clinic is the only one in town, he figured I might be able to tell him where you were staying. I gave him directions to the lighthouse."

Feeling the way Adam tensed, she stopped what she was doing. "Something wrong?"

Adam turned to face her. "Can you describe this man?"

"Let's see. Tall, maybe as tall as you, and burly. A big, barrel-chested guy with muscles out to here." She flexed her arms and held one hand over her own muscle. "Dark-haired, from what little I could see under his wool cap. I couldn't see his eyes. He was wearing sunglasses. He spoke with an accent." She was studying the frown line between Adam's eyes. "I take it you weren't expecting company?"

He shook his head. "The only one who knows I'm in Devil's Cove is my boss at WNN, and he doesn't look anything like the man you just described."

He stood and began to pull on his shirt. "Sorry,

Marcella, but I have to cut this session short. I need to make some phone calls right now.''

She picked up her appointment book. ''What about your next session?''

He was already striding across the room. ''It'll have to wait.''

He was halfway down the street when Sidney caught up with him. ''Hey. Remember me?'' She looped her arm through his and smiled up into his face. Seeing the tight line of his mouth she paused. ''What's wrong, Adam?''

''Nothing, I hope.'' He surprised her by stopping in front of the small office of the Devil's Cove Police Department.

Inside, after requesting a meeting with Police Chief Boyd Thompson, Adam and Sidney stepped into the chief's office.

After shaking hands, Boyd said, ''The Federal authorities filled me in on your background. I take it you're the only witness to the bombing, and you've already escaped two attempts on your life.''

Adam nodded. ''That's why I can't take any chances.''

Boyd sat with hands folded atop his desk and listened in silence to Adam's report of the suspected break-in at the lighthouse. It was clear, by his respectful demeanor and occasional nod, that he was taking this very seriously.

''I've been told to watch for any strangers in

town.'' Boyd arched an eyebrow. "I wonder how he found Marcella.''

"He would have known that I'd need therapy. His first botched attempt on my life occurred when he assumed the role of a doctor and nearly got to me in the hospital. If it hadn't been for the quick thinking of an emergency-room nurse, he'd have succeeded. But he was able to get his hands on my medical file.''

"I see. Okay. I'll let Mrs. Maddox and the Feds deal with the lighthouse. I'll interview Marcella and see if I can jog her memory for a better description. You realize it could just be some business associate, a reporter or fellow photojournalist you've met on your world travels, who wants to pay a call while he's in town.''

Adam shook his head. "I'm a lone wolf. My job dictates that I travel light and I travel alone.''

The minute the words were out of his mouth he wanted to snatch them back. Too late he realized that the look in Sidney's eyes wasn't so much pain as resignation.

Adam pulled his gaze away from hers and turned to the chief. "Trust me. I don't have any business associates who'd break into my place while I was gone.''

Boyd steepled his fingers atop his desk and stared right back. "You didn't say where you were when this break-in occurred.''

"I spend a lot of time in the forest, photographing nature. That's what the historical society hired me to do while staying at the lighthouse."

"Quite the woodsman, I see. You sleep in the forest?"

Adam's tone sharpened. "Where I sleep…"

Sidney laid a hand on his sleeve before turning to the police chief. "Adam spent the night at my cabin, Boyd. We just discovered the break-in this morning, when we returned to the lighthouse together."

Adam closed a hand over hers. "That's none of his business."

"It is now." Sidney's words were spoken softly but firmly.

Boyd Thompson cleared his throat. "Sorry. But Sidney's right. I need all the facts. I'll get on this right away."

Sidney gave him a smile. "Thank you, Boyd."

Though the two men shook hands, there was a strained silence between them.

Boyd remained at his desk, watching through narrowed eyes as Adam and Sidney exited his office. Then, his mind going a million miles an hour, he picked up the phone and began to dial.

It wasn't often the Federal authorities were willing to involve a small-town police chief in one of their cases. In the years since Boyd had inherited the position from his father, this was the first time that he'd been invited to play in the big leagues.

He wasn't about to let this one get away.

Chapter 13

As soon as they were outside Adam gathered Sidney close and looked down into her eyes. "I'm sorry about that. I know how you hate to be the object of town gossip, and now I've added fuel to the fire."

"Adam." She lifted a hand to his cheek. "There are no secrets in a town this small. If it hadn't been Boyd Thompson, it would have been someone else."

"You didn't have to answer him. It was none of his…"

She pressed a finger to his lips. "If we want him to do his job, we have to be honest with him."

"Hurting you wasn't part of the bargain."

"My feelings aren't important right now. Catching a killer is.'' She tucked her arm through his. ''You'll want to get back to the lighthouse.''

''The Feds need time for a thorough investigation. They asked me to stay away until they give me a report. Since there's no point in rushing, we may as well have lunch in town.''

''Are you sure?''

''Positive.'' He nodded. ''Where's the best place for lunch?''

''The Daisy Diner. Home cooking, and Carrie Lester's sweet smile.''

''Sounds like a winner.'' He allowed her to lead the way.

The diner looked the same as it had when it had been built more than forty years earlier. A small, neat wooden building with windows along one side and a large, gleaming kitchen with a stainless counter and red-leather stools for those who didn't want to sit in the booths.

A bell sounded as they opened the door to the diner. Inside they were greeted by the smell of onions on the grill and the low hum of voices, which seemed to go silent as soon as they walked in.

''Sidney.'' The blonde behind the counter hurried over with a smile. ''I don't see you nearly often enough.''

''I know. Carrie Lester, I'd like you to meet Adam Morgan.''

"Hi, Adam. How are you enjoying our lighthouse?"

He shared a knowing glance with Sidney. "I see what you mean. No secrets in this town." He turned to Carrie. "It's quite a change from what I've been used to."

Sidney caught Carrie's left hand and studied the expensive diamond that winked in the light. "When are you and Prentice tying the knot?"

"Next month. I still can't quite believe it." Carrie spoke the words on a whisper before taking the pencil from behind her ear as they settled themselves at the counter. "What'll you two have?"

After recommending the daily special and taking their order, Carrie filled two cups with steaming coffee and left them alone.

Adam leaned close. "Why can't she believe she's getting married?"

"Carrie is a single mother of an eight-year-old daughter. Prentice Osborn is one of the wealthiest men in town. He's loved Carrie since their high-school days, but was too shy to admit it, especially since he thought she was in love with someone else. And now, after all these years..."

"The proverbial happy ending." He winced. "I'm shocked, I tell you. Amazed. You actually do live in Camelot."

She gave his arm a playful slap. "Stop that."

Despite his light tone, Sidney was aware of Adam

glancing around the crowded diner, scanning the faces for anyone who might fit Marcella's description. Her light mood was gone in an instant.

When he caught Sidney watching him, he asked, "See anyone you don't know?"

She nodded at friends and neighbors before turning away. "Not a stranger in the bunch."

Adam sighed. "I don't know whether to be annoyed or relieved."

"I know what you mean."

When Carrie set their food in front of them, Adam fell silent as he tucked into thick slices of meat loaf and garlic mashed potatoes.

When he'd polished off every bite, he leaned close to mutter, "You weren't kidding about home cooking. Only this is much better than the stuff I grew up with. I've never tasted meat loaf like this."

Sidney nodded, and hoped he wouldn't notice the way she pushed the food around her plate. Her appetite had suddenly fled. "Carrie's mom has been making some of this food since I was in grade school. She still bakes all the pies, because they can't find anyone else who comes close."

"Does she make pecan pie?"

"Of course. It's one of the specialties of the house."

After polishing off a generous slice of pecan pie, Adam sat back with a sigh. "Where have they been hiding this little gem?"

Sidney shook her head. "It's obvious that you're new in town. It's no secret around here. Everybody in Devil's Cove visits the Daisy Diner at least once a week."

"Here you are." A stick-thin woman in an over-size plaid wool jacket, her white curls flattened by a band attached to earmuffs, strode into the diner and came to a halt in front of Adam. "I'm Estelle Maddox. I heard you'd come in here for lunch."

"Of course you did, Mrs. Maddox." Another look passed between Adam and Sidney, and though they shared a quick smile at the shared joke, they were just as quickly sobered by the thought of the reason for her visit. "What did you find at the light-house?"

"Nothing." She pulled several sheets of paper from her pocket and pointed to the computer-generated list. "There wasn't a single item of value to the historical society that was missing. Fred Hin-gle, that's our locksmith," she explained to Adam, "came out and replaced the lock with a dead bolt, since your...visitor was able to get in without mak-ing so much as a scratch on the old one. Here's your new key." She handed it over just as the police chief strode into the diner.

After glancing around he walked up to Adam. "You heard that nothing's missing?"

Adam nodded.

"The Feds have finished up at the lighthouse.

They said they'd keep a close watch on it, since they expect your intruder to be back. In the meantime, I have a pretty clear picture of the man who asked directions of Marcella Trowbridge. She's working with one of the Federal officer's artists. We should have flyers available by the end of the day. According to the Federal investigation, whoever broke in doesn't seem to be interested in vandalism, or in stealing anything of historic value.''

''I don't think there's any doubt about the fact that he's after me personally.''

''No doubt at all. And that begs the question why he would go to all this trouble once he learned that you weren't there.'' Boyd peered at Adam. ''Why didn't he stick around and wait for you to come back so he could finish the job?''

Adam shrugged. ''Maybe he figured he'd come back later.''

''Maybe. But now that he got careless and alerted you to the fact that he'd been there, he has to know the authorities will be expecting him. The fact that he was there while you were out could mean he wanted time to go through your valuables.''

Adam shrugged. ''I don't have any.''

''None?'' The chief thought a minute. ''What about your photographic equipment? Could he have been after that?''

''Fortunately, it was all with me, in my Jeep, and later in Sidney's cabin.''

"A good thing. You've probably got a fortune in that stuff."

"I agree. But it's only valuable to a photographer. Certainly not worth breaking into a lighthouse to steal."

"You'd be surprised what drives a man to steal. Now, you give me a camera and a dozen rolls of film, and in the end, all I'd have is useless shots of sky or trees that wouldn't be worth a dime. You, on the other hand, would probably peer through that lens and detect some exotic animal in the tree, or rare bird in the sky at that precise moment, which would make the picture worth a fortune. Which is why you're the photographer and I'm the cop." Boyd gave a short laugh. "I guess that's a fancy way of saying that one man's junk is another man's treasure."

Adam's eyes narrowed slightly at the chief's words, and he felt a tingle of memory.

Seeing the look in his eye, Boyd cocked an eyebrow. "What is it?"

Adam shook his head. "Something. Something just out of reach in my mind. It's gone now."

"If it comes back, call me. I've been told to lend a hand with the Federal investigation and help them keep a close eye on the lighthouse." Boyd turned away, touching a hand to the pistol at his hip. There was a swagger to his step that hadn't been there before.

Over his shoulder he called, "If you think of anything at all, no matter how insignificant, give a holler."

"Right. Thanks." As the chief walked out, Adam pulled himself back from his thoughts and, remembering his manners, turned to Mrs. Maddox. "Could I buy you lunch?"

"Oh, no thank you, Adam." She gave him her best smile. "After I make my report to the committee, I'm heading out to the cider mill. I promised cider and doughnuts to the historical society tonight. I'm sure our meeting will be especially lively when I make my report on all that's transpired since you arrived in town."

He gave her a faint smile. "Always happy to add a little spice to life, Mrs. Maddox."

"You've certainly done that." She gave Sidney a long, considering look before turning away.

When she was gone Adam stared after her with a solemn expression.

Sidney touched a hand to his. "What's wrong, Adam?"

"I'm beginning to think that nobody around here realizes the seriousness of this. To your police chief this is a chance to flex his muscles. To the head of the historical society, it's a bit of excitement in what might otherwise be a rather dull meeting. Does nobody understand that this is a matter of life or death?"

"Don't blame them, Adam." She kept her voice soft, so nobody would overhear. "I wasn't willing to accept it, either, when you first told me. You do have to admit that this is the last place you'd expect to find a professional killer lurking."

Professional killer. Just saying those words aloud had her throat going dry. She still found it hard to believe this was happening.

After paying for their lunch, Adam and Sidney called goodbye to Carrie and walked outside. There was a bite to the wind that had them turning up their collars until they'd reached the warmth of the Jeep.

As Adam helped Sidney inside, he glanced at the duffel lying on the floor behind his seat and thought again about what Boyd Thompson had said.

More jumbled, disconnected images filled his brain. As he drove through town he fell silent, deep in thought.

When they came to the cutoff that led to the lighthouse, Adam slowed down. "Are you in a hurry to get home?"

Sidney nodded. "I really ought to. Poor Picasso and Toulouse have been locked up all day. Do you mind?"

"Not at all." He continued along the path toward her cabin. "I'll take you home, but then I have to head back. There's something I need to do."

"All right." She studied the grim set of his mouth. "What is it, Adam?"

He shrugged. "It's something the chief said. About my photographic equipment."

"You think the assassin wants it?"

"Not the equipment. The film. I have dozens of rolls of undeveloped film, and some of them had to be taken at the time of the car bombing."

Her eyes widened as understanding dawned. "You'll call the chief and tell him what you suspect?"

He nodded. "On my way back to the lighthouse."

When they rolled to a stop in front of the cabin, they saw the dog and cat peering anxiously out the window.

"Poor babies," Sidney muttered as Adam came around to help her to the ground. "They've been cooped up too long. They look positively frazzled."

As soon as the door was unlocked Picasso and Toulouse came rushing out, dancing around while yelping and meowing.

"They're not used to being left alone for such a long time." Sidney paused on the threshold. "Will you come back for dinner?"

Adam shook his head. "The Feds will be calling all the shots until the assassin is caught. If they think I should leave the lighthouse, you know I'll be here." He drew her into his arms and kissed her. Then for good measure, he kissed her again.

Against her mouth he muttered, "As soon as I know anything, I'll call you."

Sidney waved as he climbed into the Jeep and drove away, then let herself inside, trailed by Picasso and Toulouse. With any luck, she thought, Adam would have the answer to the puzzle, and the authorities could finally track down the hired gunman before he could make good on his threats.

Adam straightened and rolled his shoulders. The last batch of negatives had been developed. Completed prints were hung to dry. Now he needed to find out if his theory was correct, and learn if he might have been unwittingly harboring the answer to this puzzle all along.

He lifted the magnifier to the prints and began studying them in minute detail. Almost at once he was thrust back into the chaos of that terrible day, hearing the chest-pounding explosion, feeling the ground shudder as the limousine burst into flame. While everyone else had begun to run away, instinct had taken over and he'd run toward the source of the fire, camera in hand, reflexively clicking off shot after shot as pieces of the vehicle exploded. Doors, windows, wheels, motor parts were flying everywhere with enough force to destroy anything in their path. The bodies of the ambassador and his assistant were flung through the air like rag dolls, falling broken and bloody hundreds of yards from the car. Even when the second explosion ripped through what remained of the limousine, Adam had continued shooting until he was thrown backward by the force of it and rendered unconscious by the jagged pieces of metal and glass that pierced his flesh, nearly severing his arm from his shoulder.

He remembered the excruciating pain as his head smashed against the pavement. Could even recall the last thought that had come unbidden to his mind, just before the darkness took over. He could have run like the others, and been safe. He could have, but didn't. And he knew with certainty that if he were given the chance to do it over, he'd do the same thing again.

If his life stood for anything, it wasn't about his own safety, but about recording the atrocities committed by those who chose to take justice into their own hands.

Once in the ambulance, as they sped to the hospital amid screaming sirens, the emergency crew had to pry the camera from Adam's hands. He could remember it now. His fingers had curled tightly around it and seemed frozen in place, as though even his subconscious mind refused to turn over control of his precious treasure.

Upon his release weeks later, his belongings had been returned to him. They consisted of his camera, his wallet and one bloody shoe, which were the only things that had survived intact. At the time, they had held no special significance to him. Now, as the memories came rushing back, he knew, with absolute certainty, that he would find what he was looking for in these negatives.

He ran a hand over his face, feeling the beads of sweat. He hadn't realized how stressful it would be to develop a simple roll of film. After all, he'd spent years recording the horrors of wars and terrorist activities. He prided himself on being able to detach himself from the violence in order to study the pictures in great detail, to determine which ones would be broadcast around the world and which would be discarded. But none of those photos had ever carried the emotional impact of these. This time, he hadn't been a mere observer, but had become, in a split second, a victim, as well.

Not a victim, he told himself, and pressed a palm to his aching shoulder as if to calm the pain that flared. He'd survived. And would continue to do so. He'd be damned if he'd let a madman win.

He studied the blurred image in the last photo. Despite the flames and the flying debris, the body parts and the chaos created by the car bomb, Adam could make out a face, peering through the waves of heat, directly into his lens.

He knew, in one sudden, chilling instant, that this was the face of the one who'd carried out the bombing. And he had no doubt whatever that it would also prove to be the face of the man who had asked directions from Marcella. The same man who had broken into the lighthouse in search of this damning evidence, in order to destroy it before it could be used against him.

Adam sat back, idly rubbing his shoulder. His own equipment might be crude, but the Federal authorities would have no problem using the latest high-tech equipment to remove all the extraneous images and bring the face into sharp relief.

That done, they would have a face that would be broadcast around the world, putting the assassin on notice that they knew what he looked like. It was only a matter of time before they would learn his identity and alert the whole world.

Adam felt a moment of jubilation. But only a moment.

Now that he had proof of what the intruder had been searching for, it was critical that he get this information to the authorities. With evidence this crucial, the assassin would stop at nothing to see that it was destroyed before it could be used against him.

He needed to get this to the authorities immediately. But first he would pick up Sidney and insist that she accompany him. Once they were both safely away from here, he would breathe a little easier.

He shoved everything inside a manila envelope and dropped it in his duffel with his equipment. With the duffel bag in one hand and his cell phone in the other, he hurried out to the Jeep.

Chapter 14

"Picasso. Toulouse." Sidney had no more than stepped into the cabin when the dog and cat pushed their way past her, almost tripping her in their haste. "What's wrong with you two?"

Picasso ran to the window and stood on his hind legs, peering out while Toulouse leaped to the countertop and practically climbed into Sidney's arms as she set down her keys.

She picked up the cat and buried her face in its fur for a moment before crossing to the fireplace to add a log to the hot coals. As flames began to lick along the bark, she settled herself in a chair. When she did, Picasso ran to her and gave a little yelp, before racing back to the window.

"I think I understand." She petted the cat and called softly, "Come here, Picasso."

Obediently, the dog walked over to rest his head on her lap.

She scratched behind his ears. "I think you two are feeling left out because of all the time I've been spending with Adam. Is that it? Are you jealous?"

Picasso licked her hand, then restlessly hurried back to the window. Refusing to settle down, Toulouse followed.

Sidney shrugged. "It could be that I'm all wrong about this. Maybe you're not jealous at all. Maybe you're just eager for Adam to return." She gave a little sigh as she made her way to the kitchen and put the kettle on for tea. "If that's the case, I understand completely. I miss him, too. The minute he's gone, I find myself missing him. Not very wise, I know. He's made it perfectly clear that he has no intention of staying in Devil's Cove. I'm trying to prepare myself for what it will feel like when he leaves, but it's impossible. I can't even imagine such a thing."

Picasso gave a low growl, deep in his throat. Hearing it, Sidney walked up beside him to peer through the window at the gathering darkness. "What do you see? Is that pesky old squirrel back again? I'll bet you're itching to get out so you can chase him home." She started toward the door.

''Come on. I think you both need some fresh air. You've been cooped up so long you're stir-crazy.''

Before she could turn the lock Picasso raced to the door and began barking. Startled, Sidney stepped back.

Her eyes narrowed as she studied the dog's unusually aggressive behavior. ''It isn't a squirrel, is it?'' She dropped to her knees to silence him. ''There's someone out there, isn't there, boy?''

The dog whimpered, and she sought to comfort him as she strained to hear anything out of the ordinary. With brittle leaves being stirred by a wild wind, it was impossible to hear anything.

Sidney's heart was pounding so hard she wondered that it didn't burst clear through her chest. How could she hope to hear anything over that frantic drumbeat at her temples?

Fear gripped her by the throat, making it impossible to swallow.

What if the assassin had somehow followed Adam here and was out there right now?

But why? If he'd watched Adam leave, wouldn't he have made a move to stop him, or at least follow him? There would be no reason for a hired gunman to lurk outside her cabin.

Picasso suddenly raced from the room and began another series of frantic barking in her bedroom.

Sidney was halfway there when she heard the sound of breaking glass. The dog lunged, emitting a feral snarl. This was something Sidney had never heard before. A man's curses filled the air a moment before the sharp crack of gunfire sounded. After a single yelp of pain, there was only an eerie silence.

Sidney's poor heart nearly stopped. Though she was desperate to know what had happened to her dog, she knew without a doubt that she had to run for her life.

With terror clogging her throat and tears stinging her eyes, she tore open the cabin door and raced headlong into the darkness.

''Thanks, Chief Thompson.'' While he spoke into his cell phone, Adam maneuvered the Jeep along the darkened trail. ''If you'll contact the Feds, I'll get this print to you as soon as I get Sidney. I'm on my way to pick her up now.''

He disconnected and tucked the phone into his breast pocket. Snowflakes speared against the windshield. The night air had grown bitter, and Adam cranked up the heater, grateful for its warmth.

He should have insisted that Sidney stay with him at the lighthouse, but the truth was, he'd feared for her safety there. Even though authorities were watching the place around the clock, this was a hired assassin they were after. A professional killer. A man like that would have no problem slipping past whatever safety measures had been put into place.

Sidney was better off here, safely tucked away in

her woods. It gave him a measure of comfort to think about her snug and safe in her cabin, happily feeding her pets and awaiting his return.

The bitter air had Sidney's teeth chattering as she raced headlong through the woods. The bare branches of trees snagged her hair as she ran. Without a parka, her thin sweater offered no protection from the cold. Her first thought had been to run toward the lighthouse. But she'd heard the snap of branches behind her, and knew that the man who'd broken into her cabin and fired that gunshot was close behind. The last thing she wanted to do was lead a hired gunman directly to Adam. Instead, she veered off, heading toward the shoreline where she had so often worked. It was a trail she was familiar with. She only hoped the man who was trailing her wasn't familiar with it, as well.

What would she do when she came to the water's edge? She had no plan. The water was too cold for a body to survive for more than a few minutes. She thought about the rotted old boat hidden under the cover of vines and shrubbery that she'd often used as a background in her paintings. Perhaps, with any luck, she could shove it into the water and make her escape. Of course, there was a good chance that it was no longer seaworthy, and would sink as soon as it left shore. She refused to dwell on that thought as she continued running, even though her lungs were burning from the effort.

She never saw the log that tripped her. One moment she was racing toward the black water up ahead, where she could see a ribbon of moonlight trailing across the waves. The next she was tumbling through space, sprawling facedown in a cushion of wet leaves and pine needles. Dazed, disoriented, she struggled to her feet, only to feel strong fingers tangle in her hair. Her head was tugged backward with such force, she fell. Before she could regain her footing, a rough hand closed around her upper arms, dragging her to her feet. She kicked out and heard a grunt of pain. Turning, she managed to twist free. Before she had taken two steps she felt something heavy slam against her temple. With stars flashing before her eyes, she crumpled to the ground.

As Adam's Jeep approached the cabin he began to relax. Just seeing the warm glow of lights through the windows had him unclenching his jaw, though he knew he wouldn't be able to relax completely until the man in the photo had been identified and captured.

He was still a few yards from the cabin when he caught sight of the door standing open, light spilling into the darkness.

He swore viciously as he slammed out of the Jeep and raced inside, shouting Sidney's name.

He was greeted by the shrill whistling of a kettle. He was across the room in quick strides. As he lifted the kettle, he realized the water had almost all boiled away.

With the kettle silenced, he became aware of a piteous meowing. Following the sound he walked to the bedroom and peered cautiously inside.

What he saw had his heart sinking. Toulouse was hovering over the still, bloody form of Picasso. The cat was licking the dog's head, as though attempting to rouse him. Wind blowing through the shattered window sent the curtains billowing inward.

Adam was sprinting toward the front door, reaching for the cell phone in his pocket, when Sidney stepped through the doorway.

"Sid..." Adam's voice trailed off, his elation short-lived.

A man was standing directly behind her, one arm wrapped around her throat, the other holding a gun to her temple.

"Well, well, Mr. Morgan." The voice was deep, and heavily accented. "Just the fish I was hoping to catch. You'll drop that phone, if you want this pretty little lure to live."

Adam hesitated for only a moment before letting his phone fall to the floor.

He saw the blood on the side of Sidney's face and the fear and pain in her eyes, and felt his own heart contract with fury. Danger and all its attendant fear

had become a way of life for him. But a woman like
Sidney had lived a lifetime sheltered from such horrors. He had been the one to bring them into her
home, and into her life.

Fear mingled with fury. He would have given
anything in the world to spare her this. And now,
he would do everything in his power to at least spare
her life.

"Let her go. She has nothing to do with this."

"She has everything to do with it. Once I realized
that she meant something to you, I knew I'd found
the key to getting what I want."

Adam avoided looking at Sidney, instead staring
directly into the man's eyes. "What if I were to tell
you she means nothing whatever to me?"

The stranger threw back his head and gave a chilling laugh. "You think on your feet. I'd have expected nothing less from a fool who would rush into
a blazing inferno just to snap a few photographs."
His smile faded. "But I know you're lying. When I
saw her photographs in your darkroom, I knew the
two of you were lovers." He moved the barrel of
his handgun across her cheek like a caress. "Only
a lover would see through his camera what you saw
through yours."

Sidney couldn't hide the shudders that rippled
through her at the touch of his gun on her flesh.
"What is it he wants, Adam?"

"Tell your lover what she wants to know." He

looked over at Adam. "I think you've guessed by now."

"That's right. I have." Adam knew he needed to keep this man talking as long as possible, until he could figure out how to save Sidney. His own life no longer mattered to him, as long as he could save her. He knew he would never again know happiness if anything happened to the woman he loved.

The woman he loved.

She could die here today without ever knowing how he truly felt about her, because he'd selfishly kept his feelings to himself, thinking to guard his heart.

"I'm sorry for bringing this trouble to your doorstep, Sidney. I had no right. But I swear to you I didn't even know about it. I'd lost all memory of what I'd done at the moment of the explosion."

"Adam, don't..."

He lifted a hand. "I just need you to know that whatever happens here, I love you."

Sidney felt tears spring to her eyes. Not just because of his declaration of love, but because of the finality of it. He knew, as she did, that they had little chance of making it away from this madman alive.

"I love you, too, Adam."

"How touching." The stranger tightened his grasp on her throat, drawing back his arm and cutting off her breath. "Tell me about the thing I'm searching for."

Adam kept his tone conversational, as though speaking to Sidney alone. "It was something the police chief said when he was talking about taking rolls of photos that triggered a memory." He remained where he was, gauging the distance between himself and Sidney. Between himself and the man who would stop at nothing to have what he wanted, even if it meant killing them both. "There was something I'd spotted through the smoke and flames while snapping photos of the car bombing. But in the confusion that followed, after I'd been so badly wounded that I was in and out of consciousness for days, I'd forgotten all about it. Until now."

"So, you do know." The man's voice was a low growl of anger.

Adam nodded. "I do now. When I developed the film, I saw a face staring directly at me through the screen of fire and debris. The FBI will be able to enhance the film enough to identify you to the whole world."

"You will give me the prints and the negatives now." For emphasis, the man pressed the pistol to Sidney's temple and curled his finger around the trigger.

"It's out in my Jeep."

The man huffed out a breath. "And you think me so stupid that I would allow you to go out there, giving you a chance to run for help."

Adam shrugged. "You can't blame a guy for trying."

The man fisted a hand in Sidney's hair, pulling her head back sharply until she gave a hiss of pain. "Your pretty little lover here will fetch the pictures." He pressed his face close to her ear. "And if you should entertain the idea of running, it will cost this fool his life."

Adam forced his tone to remain unemotional. "I'm a dead man anyway."

"Indeed you are. But if you offer no resistance, I may let the woman live to accompany me, at least until I'm safely out of town. Then…" He gave a negligent shrug of his shoulders. "Perhaps, if she pleases me, I'll take her along." His tone sharpened. "Tell her where to find the photos."

"They're in a manila folder, in my duffel bag. Sidney, remember what I said. I'm a dead man anyway. But you…"

Before he could say more the gunman calmly took aim and fired. The force of the bullet, fired at such close range, pierced Adam's shoulder and drove him back against the wall, spattering it with his blood. He slid helplessly to the floor and lay in an ever-widening pool of his own blood.

Sidney let out a series of piercing screams as she broke free of the man's arms and hurled herself across the room, taking Adam into her arms and rocking him. "Oh, Adam," she crooned. "Oh, my poor darling..."

The gunman caught her by the hair and yanked her to her feet. "I did that so that you'd know I mean business." His voice was a sinister hiss. "Bring me the photos. And if you decide to try any heroics, your lover will die. Not quickly, I guarantee you. But slowly and painfully. Do you understand?"

She saw Adam give a quick shake of his head, and she looked away. She knew what he was trying to tell her. He wanted her to run. She knew, just as strongly, that it was something she couldn't possibly do. Though her heart was thundering so painfully it felt as though it would burst clear through her chest, she knew without a doubt that she would never run to safety while the man who owned her heart was left to face this monster alone.

The stranger gave her a rough shove into the darkness and took aim at her back. As she stumbled toward the Jeep she looked around wildly for something, anything that might be used against a man with a gun.

She was rifling through Adam's duffel bag when she had a sudden thought. At first she dismissed it as being too simple. But, she realized, desperate situations called for desperate measures, and this was all she had.

As she started back to the cabin she clutched the

manila folder tightly and prayed for the courage to see this through.

She stepped through the doorway and caught sight of Adam's face. She saw the look of absolute disbelief in his eyes, along with the despair.

''Sidney.'' She heard the note of betrayal in his voice.

''I know what you wanted, Adam, but I couldn't leave you.'' She held out the manila folder.

As the man reached for it, he caught sight of the camera she was cradling to her chest.

He looked more annoyed than alarmed. ''What are you...''

She snapped a picture, causing a sudden, blinding flash.

Using that moment of distraction Adam was on his feet and diving for the gunman, driving him back against the wall. As the two men wrestled for control of the gun it slipped from the stranger's hand and slid across the floor.

Before either man could reach it, Sidney was there, picking it up gingerly before backing away. Her hand was trembling so violently, she nearly dropped it.

She watched in horror as the stranger's fist slammed into Adam's midsection, causing him to crumple in pain. As he fell to the floor the man was on him, pummeling him with his fists, driving his head against the wall again and again until Adam slumped backward, barely conscious.

The stranger sprang up and turned to Sidney. "Give me the gun."

"Never." The word was little more than a strangled whisper.

Seeing the way she was trembling, the man gave a knowing smile. "Look at you. So brave. And all for the sake of your lover. All right then, go ahead and shoot me."

When she made no move, he took a step toward her. "In the right hands, a gun can be a powerful weapon. But in the hands of a frightened little coward like you, it's nothing more than a toy." He gave a laugh of triumph. "I think I'll have to take your toy away from you now."

As he started toward her she began backing up like one in a trance, using her free hand to steady the trembling hand holding the gun.

As she backed into her bedroom, the rush of frigid air was like a slap in the face. She blinked, and realized with cold finality that there was no place left to run.

"Now we have the moment of truth," the stranger taunted as he reached out a hand toward her. "I don't believe you have the will to use that toy."

In that instant there was a low, feral snarl, as a blur of gray fur launched through the air, grabbing the man by the throat and taking him backward with the force of a missile.

The stranger gave a cry of pain as he struggled to shove the dog aside. Hearing a yelp, the frightened cat went into action, hissing and spitting. With Picasso clinging tenaciously to the stranger's throat, and Toulouse scratching at his eyes, Sidney began beating the man over the head with the pistol until he was forced to cover his head with his arms and curl into a ball to protect himself from his attackers.

Through a haze of pain Adam struggled to stand. Forcing one foot in front of the other he crossed to Sidney's side. Leaning weakly against the wall he held out his hand. ''Give me the gun, Sidney.''

Before she could do as he asked, Boyd Thompson, along with three armed men, burst into the cabin, guns drawn. When they saw the stranger on the floor, still fighting off the dog and cat, they stepped in and began to handcuff him.

In the blink of an eye there was a flurry of activity as the men began flashing pictures, bagging bits of broken glass, talking animatedly into their phones.

''Took you long enough.'' Adam could feel a buzzing in his head and knew he wouldn't be able to stand much longer.

Boyd Thompson frowned. ''We got here as fast as we could.''

Sidney turned to Adam. ''How did Boyd know to come here?''

"I hit Redial before tossing aside my phone."

The police chief nodded. "I could hear everything. Just couldn't do anything about it." He took the gun from Sidney's hand and could feel the way she was still vibrating with aftershocks. "You might want to sit down, Sidney, before your legs give out."

"Why would my legs..." She went pale and wondered if she was going to faint.

Just then she noticed that Adam was sliding slowly to the floor. "Oh, Adam. Oh, my darling, hold on." She gathered him into her arms and rocked him, feeling his blood soak through her sweater and stain her flesh.

At once, Picasso and Toulouse were there, licking Adam's face, then Sidney's, as if to assure themselves that they were indeed safe.

As his deputies led the stranger from the cabin, Boyd glanced out the window and saw the headlights moving along the lane. "That would be the ambulance. The Feds ordered one, just in case there were casualties."

"...hospital." Adam could feel his strength ebbing.

"Yes. As fast as possible." Sidney hovered as a team of medics assessed his wounds and administered a sedative before wheeling him toward the waiting vehicle.

As Sidney climbed in behind him, the dog and cat followed.

"Sorry, ma'am. You and those animals will have to..."

Adam put a hand on his sleeve and muttered thickly, "You don't want to take them on. They just overpowered a hired killer. Besides, the dog is a wounded hero. You may want the doctors to look at him, too."

"You don't say?" The medic didn't know whether to believe him or whether it was the sedative talking. At any rate, there was no time to argue, since his patient was out cold, as was the dog, and both were being tended by the woman and the cat.

He turned to the driver. "It's time to get this circus on the road."

Chapter 15

Emily, dressed in a lab coat, a stethoscope around her neck, leaned over Adam's hospital bed. "You look awful."

Adam struggled to focus through a haze. "You ought to see the other guy."

"I did. He's a mess. How do you explain those bite marks at his throat?"

"Maybe I'm really a werewolf. Isn't that one of the rumors going around town about me?"

"Mmm-hmm. But not anymore. Now they're saying you're an undercover agent, and the guy being held by Federal officers is an international terrorist."

"Some people will believe anything."

"Quiet." She took his pulse, then moved around

the bed to shine a light in Sidney's eyes, lifting first one lid, then the other.

She studied her sister, holding tightly to Adam's hand as though she might never let go. "Why are you so calm, Sid?"

Sidney sighed. "I'm fine."

"Yeah, that's what has me puzzled. At first I thought you were in shock. That's what most people would suffer after a trauma like this. I was especially concerned about you, Sid. You've always been our…fragile one. You know. The one who doesn't like stress and mess in her life. So just why are you acting so…serene?"

Sidney merely held on to Adam's hand as though her life depended on it. "I don't know. Maybe it's the new me. Calm. Controlled. Fearless now that the danger has passed."

"Just to make certain, I've asked one of our trauma specialists to drop by later and evaluate you."

"I don't need…"

Sidney looked up as Marcella Trowbridge came racing into the room and skidded to a halt.

Seeing Adam lying in bed, his wounds covered with dressings, she rubbed her hands together. "In case you haven't figured it out yet, that bullet they removed has sent you back to square one in your physical therapy."

"You're just full of good news, aren't you?"

Adam gave her a lopsided grin. "Why are you looking so gleeful?"

"Just warming up these muscles. I can't wait to
get my hands on you."

He groaned, then winked at Sidney, who grinned
back as though sharing some wonderful, silly joke.

Hearing voices in the hallway, Emily looked over
and gave a long, drawn-out sigh. "I recognize those
voices. I warned the family to stay away, but as
usual, they've decided they live by their own rules."
Under her breath she whispered, "Brace yourself,
Adam. It's the attack of the Brennans."

"Well done, son." Frank Brennan was the first
one through the door. When he reached Adam's
bedside he pumped his hand until Adam was forced
to grit his teeth against the pain. "That was some
fast thinking on your part, speed-dialing the police
chief and alerting him to the danger you and our
Sidney were in."

Charley had her daughter in a fierce bear hug and
looked as though she might never let her go. When
she finally relaxed her grip, she held Sidney a little
away to study her carefully. "Oh, my poor, sweet
darling. I've been frantic to just hold you and know
that everything's all right. You'll come home with
us and let us pamper you for a few months. Then,
when you're feeling refreshed and restored..."

Sidney stroked her mother's hair. "I'm fine,
Mom. Really."

''You're fine?'' Charley looked around at the others. ''Sidney says she's fine.''

On the other side of the bed, Bert bent to press a kiss to Adam's cheek. ''Boyd Thompson told us how you saved our Sidney.''

''It was the other way around. Sidney's quick thinking saved us both.''

''We figured you'd say that.'' Hannah nudged Ethan, who nodded in agreement.

Their two little boys, Danny and T.J., were staring at Adam as though he were a football hero.

''Really.'' Adam wondered why he was feeling so light-headed. Maybe it was the sedative. Or maybe it was that floating feeling he'd experienced at times while covering an especially dangerous assignment, when the adrenaline rush was over. ''You should have seen Sidney. She was amazing.''

''Did you cry, Aunt Sidney?'' Danny asked.

''Of course not.'' She huffed out a breath. ''Well, I would have, but there wasn't time.''

''You're crying now.'' Danny reached into his pocket and removed a clean handkerchief, before handing it to her.

Sidney wiped it over her eyes, then blew her nose. ''These are happy tears.''

Trudy pushed her way through the crowd to stand at the bedside, staring down at Adam. Her rusty-gate voice was trembling with emotion. ''I knew you were hero material the first time I met you.''

"I told you, I'm no hero." He turned to Sidney. "Make them listen."

She merely smiled. "The Brennan family is known for hearing only what they choose to hear."

"Yeah, that's what I'm beginning to understand." He leaned back against the pillows, watching the crowd gathering around his bed as though watching a sitcom on television. Their voices a chorus of high and low, soft and rough, anxious and teasing as they hugged one another, touched, whispered, nodded, laughed.

He turned to Sidney's grandfather. "I'm really sorry, Frank. You were right. I brought that madman right to Sidney's door. My fault."

"Hush now," the old man said. "Not another word of apology, do you hear?"

"Adam, look." Courtney signaled for her husband Blair to turn up the volume on the hospital TV. "You're on the news."

For a moment they all fell silent as the news anchor showed file photos of Adam as he'd looked in half a dozen different countries while on assignment for WNN, sporting a beard in some, hair long and tied back in a ponytail in others, his eyes hard and fierce or bleary from lack of sleep, his voice edged with excitement, while at other times the words seemed slurred from sheer exhaustion.

"Wow." Courtney fanned herself with her hand. "You were some hunk."

"Were?" Adam winked at Sidney. "She makes me sound like a faded shadow of my former self."

"Okay. I admit, you're still a hunk. Almost as hunky as my man here." Courtney draped an arm around Blair's shoulders as they drew close to watch and listen in rapt silence.

The screen was filled with photos of the stranger, identified as an international terrorist who had carried out the car bombing that killed a foreign ambassador and his assistant while in New York several months earlier, as well as being a suspect in several other assassination attempts in foreign countries. In broken English he spoke angrily of the man and woman, and even a mad dog, that had foiled his attempt to steal the proof of his guilt.

His words brought a round of cheers from those assembled around the bed in Adam's room.

"Quiet," Hannah shouted as a video of Sidney, taken at one of the first public exhibitions of her art at a gallery in New York years earlier, flashed onto the screen.

"Oh, look how cute you were," Hannah said with a laugh.

"I think she's still cute." Adam was grinning foolishly.

The others joined in laughter while Sidney merely blushed.

A nurse paused in the doorway with a bundle in

her arms. "I believe this belongs to someone in here."

Adam wondered if he were hallucinating. "Please tell me that's not a baby."

She merely laughed and set the bundle down on the bed beside him. When she opened a corner of the blanket, Picasso thrust his nose into Adam's hand.

"Well, old boy, aren't you looking fine." Adam ran a hand over Picasso's back and was rewarded with several licks of a wet tongue before Toulouse leaped onto the bed and nudged the dog aside before settling on Adam's lap, purring contentedly.

The nurse turned to Sidney. "We summoned two veterinary doctors to check our little hero. The bullet passed clear through. He was stunned, and in some pain, but he's comfortable now, and the doctors assured us that he'll be good as new in a few days. They said to warn you that your cat, however, is armed and dangerous. He sank his claws into the first doctor who attempted to examine the dog. We had to restrain him in a cage before the doctors could work on Picasso."

While the others roared with laughter, Sidney found herself weeping again, especially when her grandfather gathered her into his arms and drew her close to his chest.

"Oh, Poppie. You should have seen Picasso. He was so brave."

''From what I've heard, he wasn't the only one.''
He tipped up her quivery chin. ''My brave granddaughter deserves nothing less.'' He looked over her
head. ''Only the bravest of pets, and men, for my
brave, wonderful girl.''

She managed to smile through her tears. ''Are
you saying I'm no longer delicate and...fragile?''
She actually wrinkled her nose at that word, which
brought another round of laughter from the others.

''Not a bit of it. Why, I believe you may be the
strongest one of all the Brennans,'' her grandfather
said with pride.

Someone found a chair for Bert, who pulled it
close to Adam's bed before settling herself in it.

''Look at them.'' Her voice was a sea of calm as
she studied her family crowded around the room.
''Aren't they something?''

Adam caught her hand. ''Yeah. I was just thinking the same thing. You have an amazing family,
Bert.''

She smiled at his easy use of her nickname.
''There's always room for one more.''

He chuckled, before lifting her hand to his lips.
''You're a sly woman.''

''So I've been told.'' When he released her hand
she folded it in her lap and sat back, enjoying
the show.

Adam, she noted, seemed to be enjoying himself

immensely while Emily, ever the efficient doctor, was trying, without success, to control the chaos.

Emily turned to the nurse. "Would you mind closing that door? If word gets out that we have animals in this hospital, we'll start hearing from a dozen different patients about their allergies."

"Too late, Dr. Brennan. Word's already out. The hospital, and the whole town, is buzzing about the international conspiracy that just put Devil's Cove on the map. The place is swarming with television crews. They're hunting down anyone who has ever known Sidney and Adam, and I predict that Sidney's pets will become part of local folklore." The nurse was still laughing as she left, closing the door firmly behind her.

When he was certain they were alone, Frank Brennan produced a bottle of champagne and paper cups, which were quickly filled and passed around.

Emily tried to take the cup from Adam's hand. "You really shouldn't have this until the sedative has worn off."

"Wait a minute." Laughing, he took it back. "I earned this." He touched it to Sidney's cup. "And so did you."

As the others lifted their cups, he said softly, "Here's to the bravest woman I know. Sidney, without your quick thinking, we wouldn't have survived."

In silence they all sipped.

It was Danny's voice that broke the silence. "Weren't you afraid, Aunt Sidney?"

She nodded. "I was terrified. I've never even seen a handgun before, let alone held one. But how could I let my fear paralyze me when Adam's life hung in the balance? I knew I would either find a way for him to live, or I was going to die with him."

The sincerity of her words had the others sighing.

After clearing his throat several times, Frank was able to mutter, "That's my girl. I always knew you had the right stuff."

As the others began proposing more toasts, Adam set aside his cup.

Alarmed, Sidney leaned close. "They're tiring you out, aren't they? I'll make them leave…"

"Don't you dare."

"Adam, you don't mind…?"

He merely grinned and caught Sidney's hand, bringing it to his lips. "I think we should take a lesson from your grandmother and just enjoy the show."

Sidney glanced across the bed at the old woman who sat sipping her champagne. As their gazes met, the two women shared a secret, knowing smile.

Sidney leaned close, nuzzling her lips to Adam's ear. "Admit it. You like my family, don't you?"

"I do." He tucked an arm under his head and looked down at the dog and cat, happily asleep on the blanket. "I never had much of a family. Never had a pet, either. I think, if I play my cards right, I just might have them all.''

''You're thinking of staying?'' Sidney felt her heart skip several beats as she waited for his reply.

''How could I ever leave this? Or you?'' In his head he could hear the music from *Camelot* playing. The words of a lover, wondering how he could leave his woman in spring, summer, winter or fall.

Maybe he really had fallen under some sort of spell. Maybe Sidney Brennan really was a witch, living in an enchanted cottage. If so, he had no intention of finding a way to chase away the magic.

He knew he was wearing a silly smile. It didn't matter. He knew, too, he'd probably feel like hell in the morning when the pain medication wore off. That didn't matter, either. What did matter, more than anything in the world, was what he had right here in this room.

He wasn't going to let his very own Camelot slip away. Not if he could help it. Not now. Not ever.

Epilogue

Adam peered out the window of the lighthouse at the sea of people swarming across the leaf-covered lawn, and shook his head in dismay. "Is the whole town invited?"

"You bet." Jason Cooper, handsome in a dove-gray morning coat and striped trousers, reached for Adam's tie and knotted it. Stepping back he gave a nod of approval. "Okay. You'll pass."

"Or pass out." Adam glanced once more at the scene outside the window. The historical society, eager to showcase their lighthouse for this special occasion, had decorated the lawn, the porch and all of the rooms with masses of russet and gold and white mums, as well as gourds and pumpkins and golden shafts of wheat and corn. Hundreds of chairs, each sporting a satin bow, had been arranged in a circle, with a platform in the middle for the wedding party. Zigzagging through the crowd were Picasso and Toulouse, sporting white-satin bows of their own, and savoring all the attention they were getting from the invited guests. "What was I thinking when I agreed to this?"

"What every guy is thinking." Ethan nudged Blair and the two shared a chuckle. "We'll do whatever the little woman wants, as long as she agrees to be ours exclusively. The next thing you know, that simple little wedding ceremony turns into the event of the year."

Frank Brennan stepped into the room carrying a tray with a bottle of whiskey and five tumblers on it. He glanced around nervously before setting it down. "You'll let me know if you see Trudy coming downstairs. Right now she's up there." He nodded. "With all the females, fussing over the bride." He began filling the glasses and passing them around. "If she catches us drinking before the ceremony, she'll tell Bert. And I promised my lovely wife that I'd keep this day dignified and unsentimental."

"As if you could keep such a promise." Jason Cooper grinned at the others.

"And what's that supposed to mean?" The Judge shot him a look.

"Unsentimental? When you're presiding at your last single granddaughter's wedding? Judge, I've seen you cry at old Lassie movies."

The men roared with laughter.

"I will not shed a tear." Frank lifted a tumbler. "Gentlemen…" As that word washed over him he gave a sly grin. "Do you realize, with the addition of Adam to our family, I'm no longer outnumbered by women?"

Ethan glanced at his two sons, looking adorable in their new suits and crisp white shirts, blond hair slicked back, shoes so shiny they could see their reflections. "It took long enough, Judge."

"So it did. Better late than never. Now where was I?" Frank thought a minute. "All right. First, I'd like to propose a toast to my son, Christopher, who is surely watching from heaven and feeling so proud of his wife and daughters."

"To Christopher," the men said in unison before drinking.

"And of course, to you, Adam." Frank lifted his glass in a salute. "For bringing the sunshine back into Sidney's life."

Adam watched the others drink. "You've got it wrong, Judge. She brought the sunshine into mine."

Just then Trudy clattered down the stairs, dabbing an apron to her eyes. The men quickly formed a solid wall of bodies in front of the tray, but Trudy wasn't fooled.

Her red-rimmed eyes flashed fire. "Judge Brennan." Her words were a huff of righteous indignation. "You gave your word."

"And I'll not break it if you say so." He held up his empty tumbler to appease her. "But I was just about to ask you to join us, Trudy, in a toast to the lovely bride."

Trudy's eyes filled and she sniffed before she walked toward him. "All right. Just one." She watched as he filled it halfway. Instead of picking it up she merely looked at him, and after a moment's hesitation, he filled it to the top, before filling the others.

"To our sweet, fragile Sidney." Frank's voice faltered for just a moment before he managed to add, "I must stop saying that. Here's to our brave, courageous Sidney, who deserves, more than anyone I know, a lifetime of happiness."

Trudy sniffled before tipping up the glass and emptying it in one long swallow.

Hearing the door open upstairs, and the nervous laughter of the women, Trudy efficiently collected all the empty tumblers and set them on the tray before disappearing toward the kitchen. Over her shoulder she grumbled, "I still don't see why we couldn't have held this wedding at the Willows. I'd have had a much easier time in my own kitchen."

Adam looked up expectantly at the sound of footsteps on the stairs and felt a wave of disappointment when it wasn't Sidney, but Bert.

She paused halfway down the stairs. "All right. You men have to clear the room now. Step outside so the bride can come down."

"Wait." Adam paused at the foot of the steps. "I want to see Sidney."

"It's customary to wait until the ceremony to see the bride, Adam." Bert turned away.

He started up behind her.

Below, the Judge rolled his eyes and pulled open the front door. "Come on, gentlemen. I say we get out before the fireworks begin, or we might get hit by a rocket or two."

As he stepped out onto the porch, he waved at the crowd before saying in an aside, "Poor Adam. I'd hate to go up against Bert, Charley and those four little women. He doesn't know what he's in for."

"Oh, I don't know." Jason took up his position beside his brothers-in-law and winked at the two little boys who looked as if they'd rather be chasing after squirrels than standing at attention, holding satin pillows. "Adam's been through wars and uprisings, and faced down an international terrorist. I'm betting he can hold his own against the Brennan women."

Ethan nodded in agreement. "I'm with you, Jason."

Just then they caught sight of the women streaming down the stairs.

Blair chuckled. "They're all there except Adam and Sidney. Looks like our guy won."

Jason clapped the Judge on the shoulder. "I never had a doubt."

It had been decided by the women that the light tower would be used as a dressing room for the bride and her attendants. Several tables had been set up to hold the dozens of bottles, jars, tubes and sprays that women need for such a day. Chairs were draped with bits of clothing. Half a dozen pairs of shoes littered the floor.

In the midst of it all stood Sidney, wearing a simple column of white silk that fell in soft folds to her ankles. She wore no jewelry. No veil covered the waist-length spill of autumn hair.

She heard the hurried footsteps as Adam raced up the stairs, and felt the sudden quick tug at her heart as he stepped into the room.

"Look how handsome you are. Bert said you wanted to see me before the ceremony. Having a change of heart, Adam?"

He shook his head, unable to speak over the constriction in his throat. For the longest time he merely stood there, waiting for his heartbeat to steady and his world to settle.

At last he gave a long, deep sigh. "Sidney, you take my breath away."

"Good." She smiled, and he wondered that he wasn't blinded by the brilliance of it. "I hope you still feel that way fifty years from now."

"You can count on it." He took a step toward her. Only a step, afraid that if he moved too quickly, the vision would fade and he'd discover that this was all a dream.

"Are you sorry that our small, intimate wedding has grown into this elaborate affair?"

"I guess I was, for a minute or two. But now, I wouldn't mind if the whole world witnessed this." He stepped closer and framed her face with his hands. As he stared down into her eyes, he felt such a welling of love, he wondered that his heart didn't simply explode. "I love you, Sidney Brennan."

"And I love you, Adam Morgan."

"I received a wedding gift from WNN today."

"Really?" She looked up into his eyes. "What is it?"

"They refused to accept my resignation. Instead, when they heard about the book of wildlife photos I'm planning in conjunction with the historical society's almanac, they offered to publish it, as long as I'd expand it into a television special that they could air next year."

"You can live here and work here, and never have to leave?"

He nodded. "They said, though they're sorry to lose a good field operative, they're willing to do whatever is necessary to keep me on the staff."

"That's quite a compliment, Adam. But I'm not surprised. I knew the minute we met that you were rare and special."

"You're the one who's special, Sidney." He brushed her lips with his.

Hearing the sound of music drifting up, they walked to the wall of glass to peer at the crowd below. The entire Brennan family was gathered on the center platform, awaiting the bride and groom.

Sidney touched a hand to Adam's arm. "Look at this perfect day. I'm so glad the weather cooperated. I was afraid we might have snow. Instead, this is one of those rare autumn days that seems to glow in sunlight."

"You're the one who glows, Sidney."

She tucked her arm through his. "Ready?"

He caught her hand and lifted it to his lips. "More than ready."

Together they descended the stairs and walked out into the afternoon sunlight. As soon as they stepped out the door, Danny and T.J. steadied their satin pillows and moved along ahead of them to the delight of the crowd.

Sidney smiled at Carrie Lester and her daughter, Jenny, who were seated with Prentice Osborn and his brother, Will.

Adam winked at Marcella Trowbridge and couldn't help flexing his muscle a bit as he passed by, much to her delight.

Sidney mouthed a greeting to Skeeter Hilton and another to Claire Huntington, whose waiters from The Pier would be helping Trudy serve the wedding buffet that had been prepared by The Pier's chef.

Adam gave a thumbs-up to Mrs. Maddox and the members of the historical society, who were beaming their approval at the way their lovely jewel-of-a-historical lighthouse was being showcased by what many in town considered the wedding of the year.

As Adam helped Sidney up the steps of the platform, she paused to kiss her mother and grandmother and to hand each of them a single, long-stemmed rose. And then she was standing with Adam before her grandfather, who looked every inch a formal judge in his flowing robes.

They spoke their vows in clear voices, and sealed them with a kiss that earned the applause of everyone in attendance. They endured the handshakes of all the well-wishers and words of wisdom from their elders. They sipped champagne during the endless toasts and nibbled The Pier's fabulous trout, whitefish, prime rib and lemon chicken.

Watching them, Frank Brennan touched a finger to the tear that trickled from the corner of his wife's eye. His own eyes were a bit misty, as well. "We did it, Bert. Lived to see them all happily settled."

She nodded and looked around at their big, noisy family, laughing and dancing, hugging one another and thoroughly enjoying the celebration.

As the bride and groom stood in the center of the platform for another toast, Adam leaned close to whisper, "You know what I'm thinking about?"

Sidney gave him an impish grin. "Dessert?"

He drew her close. Against her mouth he muttered, "Absolutely. And I don't mean The Pier's cheesecake."

"Oh, Adam." She linked her arms around his neck and moved to the music they'd requested. Show tunes from *Camelot*. "I want to grow old with you."

"You'll be as wise and calm as Bert."

"And you'll be as tenderhearted and doting as Poppie."

He thought of the accident that had brought him here, and realized there were no accidents in this life. It had all been part of some grand, heavenly plan. He'd been destined to meet the most beautiful, courageous woman in the world, who would open her home, and her heart, to a stranger and would teach him the greatest lesson of all.

Sometimes the simplest things in this world, done out of love, can fill all the empty places in a heart the way nothing else can. And what could be simpler than a man, a woman and a place called home?

* * * * *

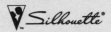

INTIMATE MOMENTS™

Introducing the gripping new miniseries

CODE of the OUTBACK

by reader favorite

VALERIE PARV

Heir to Danger
(Silhouette Intimate Moments #1312)

Desert princess Shara Najran needs evidence to prove that the man her father has chosen for her is actually out to steal the royal throne. But when her fiancé kidnaps her and takes her to Australia to force their marriage, Shara is rescued by Tom McCullough, an Outback lawman. Together Tom and Shara uncover a treacherous alliance between her fiancé and Tom's unscrupulous neighbor. Their dangerous investigation brings Tom one step closer to finding a legendary diamond mine on his family's land, and a giant step closer to losing his heart to Shara.

*Coming in August 2004
to your favorite retail outlet.*

Sparked by passion, fueled by danger.

Silhouette®

I N T I M A T E   M O M E N T S™

Every month, live the most passionate adventure of your life with six sexy heroes. In any given month, you might get the chance to...

Lose yourself in the strong arms of a cop.

Live dangerously with a prince.

Break your cover with a Navy SEAL.

Uncover corporate espionage with a sexy single CEO.

Target a secret agent. Your reward: love.

Zero in on a top gun fighter pilot's heart.

Each month, read six exciting and unforgettable stories by your favorite authors—only in Silhouette Intimate Moments.

Available at your favorite retail outlet.

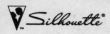

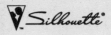

INTIMATE MOMENTS™

A thrilling new story by
BRENDA HARLEN
Bulletproof Hearts

Natalie Vaughan came to Fairweather looking for a fresh start, and her job as Assistant D.A. was a perfect new beginning. But working closely with handsome but gruff police lieutenant Dylan Creighton rattled her, as did the unwelcome spark of attraction that flared between them. And when she put herself directly in the line of fire to help take down an organized crime kingpin, she risked losing her carefully guarded heart to the cop who had vowed to protect her—at all costs.

Don't miss this compelling new book...only from Silhouette Intimate Moments.

Available at your favorite retail outlet.

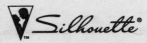

COMING NEXT MONTH